JEDIDIAH WASHINGTON

Harvey Butaleon Degree Sr.

Pollyworm Books
Shelby, North Carolina

Published by:
Pollyworm Books
Shelby, North Carolina

Cover design: Trilmatic Productions
Editing and Interior Design: Before You Publish – Book Press

First Edition: Jedidiah Washington
Degree Sr., Harvey

ISBN-13: 978-1981615636
ISBN-10: 1981615636

JEDIDIAH WASHINGTON

Chapter One

They were thirsty to convict him.
But they had to prove it first.
They, being Libertore.

Most people would like to think if they were in a life or death situation there would be that one person who would move heaven and earth to come to their rescue. Jedidiah Washington had no such person.

Jedidiah knew from the moment jury selection began that he didn't have a snowball's chance in hell of walking the streets of Carver City a free man again. The long reaching arms of Libertore had penetrated into the courthouse. Libertore planned to sandbag Jedidiah's case by giving him a dumbass public defender. A fresh-faced punk whose balls they could squeeze. Jedidiah was aware of their plan and had already made preparations. He would steer the public defender in the direction to expose Libertore. Most people believed Libertore was a myth fabricated in the nineties by a Carver City Post reporter named Jacob Ross. Ross became a legend at the paper for bringing down the Mayor, the Governor, and a few other high-profile individuals.

Jedidiah had been a reporter at the Post for almost eleven years. In that time, he worked closely with Ross and listened hours on end to him tell stories about Libertore. He'd said that if such an order as the Illuminati were to exist, the Libertore would be their equivalent.

Jedidiah flipped open the dossier in front of him and glanced over the information Ross had provided to help with his defense. It was a detailed history of how Libertore originated.

Ross had been skeptical at first, but after Garcia's sister, Shirley was murdered due to mistaken identity, he accepted her request. Together Ross and Garcia uncovered four key players. A prominent lawyer, a distinguished minister, the Governor, and Jedidiah's uncle, a gas station attendant. These Vietnam War heroes all formed a private hate club in 1975 called "Take over America."

Ross, Garcia, and a woman named Angela dug up everything needed to expose Libertore. Except the courts didn't recognize Libertore as a secret society, but as an assembly of people who got arrested doing illegal things.

Jedidiah couldn't afford an attorney so the state of North Carolina provided one for him. Henry Fowler looked to be in his early thirties, just beginning to go bald. He wore a dated pair of plastic frame glasses with thick lenses and a brown suit Jedidiah could have sworn he'd seen on sale at Fredrick's Bargain Basement. This was further proof for Jedidiah to believe this case wouldn't end in his favor.

The moment Jedidiah first laid eyes on Henry he knew the man graduated at the bottom of his law class. How did he know? When the two of them sat down for their first interview, Henry opened up his worn U. S. Luggage bag to retrieve a legal pad and found, to his surprise, it was missing. He muttered something under his breath about having left it back at the office. In need of something to take notes on, Henry placed a small notepad on the table. Next the court appointed attorney produced a cheap Papermate ink pen. Jedidiah didn't know how much the state was paying Henry to defend him but he clearly understood he should not make any type of plans, travel or otherwise, for the next twenty to thirty years. Dumb looking and unkempt as he was, Henry seemed to figure he could get Jedidiah freed.

Jedidiah wasn't stupid. It was Henry's job to say dumb shit like that. Jedidiah took a moment to study the jury. A jury of Jedidiah's peers consisted of six white men, four white women, one black man and one Hispanic woman. The two alternate jurors were white middle-aged men. The black man was three shades lighter than Jedidiah, shiny baldhead, and wore a nice expensive suit. By contrast, Jedidiah's hair was done up in dreadlocks and his clothes off the clearance rack at Kmart.

Juror five was a Hispanic woman with tattoos covering both arms in the shape of samurai swords. Beautiful teeth, gorgeous smile. Her long dark, silky hair framed her face well. She wore tight little outfits to court that made the six men on the jury pay her special attention. Her broken English made Jedidiah question if she understood enough of what the judge said.

Juror three was a man with longish white hair tied back in a ponytail. Tall and athletically built, he talked loud even when he was trying to whisper. The bailiff had to give the loud mouth the evil eye on several occasions during the first two days of jury selection. Jedidiah took the man to be the kind accustomed to talking loudly to get other's attention.

Sitting in the courtroom, being treated and painted to look like a criminal, made Jedidiah more determined than ever to expose Libertore. The Libertore, like the Free Masons and Bilderberg, is the hidden and driving force of society and currently trying to drive right over Jedidiah. Less than two weeks after confiding in his editor that he wanted to do a piece on Libertore, Jedidiah was given his walking papers. The official term for his sudden dismissal was economic downsizing. Yet, Jedidiah knew the paper was in the black. He'd stepped on the wrong toes. Before such an article was allowed to be printed, Libertore would smash him like a bug. It was pure insanity for Jedidiah to think he could trip a giant. Libertore was now going to chew him up and spit him out in a court of law as an example of their power.

Ten months passed without Jedidiah finding employment. Interviewers seemed optimistic at first but most of them never gave him a call back. Of those that did, he was told the position had been filled. Jedidiah knew, but couldn't prove, Libertore was the reason he was being blackballed. Yet he continued to talk about Libertore to anyone who would listen.

A sudden motion caused Jedidiah to turn his attention back to the jury. Juror nine was bent over picking something up he had dropped in front of him. He was a man so damn skinny that if he were to skip lunch on a windy day, they would never see him again. He stood about five-six or five-seven with blond hair cut rather short. When Jedidiah looked him in the face, he felt the wrongs of the universe competing for the man's soul.

Juror four was a woman with short-styled gray hair, streaked with diminishing shades of black. Jedidiah couldn't help but notice how genuinely polite she had been during the selection process and thought for certain the prosecutor would dismiss her. Try as he may, Jedidiah couldn't see her returning a guilty verdict with such flimsy evidence the state had against him.

Juror eleven was a man with a shiny baldpate and a full Abe Lincoln-type beard. It was clear he didn't want to be sitting between jurors ten and twelve. Jedidiah assumed he would subject his misery against him. If not for Jedidiah's trial, the man wouldn't be here.

Juror seven was a woman who was a real looker all right, only thing, she wasn't looking at Jedidiah. Each time Jedidiah tried to make eye contact with her she would quickly turn back to face the judge.

Juror eight was a man appearing to be the same age as Jedidiah, roughly the same height and body weight, and even dressed like him. The man wore a wedding band but that didn't stop him from eyeballing the young female Assistant District Attorney. Jedidiah had to agree; she was definitely eye candy. But the young woman's plans for his future didn't include freedom.

Juror two was the lone black man whose narrow-slit eyes looked upon Jedidiah as if he was a disgrace to the black race. He never tried to hide his contempt. It was bad apples like Jedidiah who kept uppity Negroes like number two awake at night worrying about how his Caucasian coworkers per-ceived the apple barrel.

****

The man Jedidiah was accused of killing was a Do-minican Republic immigrant named Salvador Alfred Her-nandez. Hernandez's street name was El Fuego Del Diablo *The Fire of the Devil.* Folks went silent at the name.

Over the years, bodies had been found with their throats sliced or their tongues cut out. None of it could be pinned on Diablo El Fuego but they could, however, all be linked to him. On the surface, Sal Hernandez was owner of a midscale fish market on Clancy Street next to the pier. Whale of a Fish Market was on the radar of every intelligence team in the country. Carver City Narcotics officers suspected that Hernandez moved drugs and weapons using his fleet of fishing ships, but raided after the sting came up empty.

Carver City police, the year before, had unwisely planted two undercover detectives inside Diablo's fish market. Within months, both men were hacked in pieces and packaged before being shipped first class delivery back to their precincts. This deed of audacity made it imperative to the mayor and the police commissioner that Sal Hernandez was to be taken down. But now that Hernandez was dead, city leaders were going all out to prove it wasn't one of their own that had done the deed. The dead man's widow filed a massive lawsuit against the city, claiming it was a hit. After Jedidiah was arrested, little effort was spent looking elsewhere for a killer.

Jedidiah stole a glance back over his shoulder. Immediately, he recognized Hector *Cockroach* Gomez and Juan *Moose Dung* Montana, heavy muscle for Hernandez and known to be his top two lieutenants. By now one of them was running the fishing enterprise. Montana was dressed in a flowery short sleeve shirt like he just stepped out of a bad episode of *Burn Notice*. The sorry turd was nothing more than a Hollywood gangster. Jedidiah laughed at the thought.

Suddenly Jedidiah had another inspiration that wasn't so funny. If he were to beat the state's charges against him— *what would his life be worth on the street?* Somewhere, sometime, someone was going to pay for the death of El Fuego Del Diablo. The Dominicans would see to that. Being found not guilty in court didn't make him innocent on the street.

Ask O.J. Simpson.

One thing Jedidiah could attest to—living behind bars was hell. Every second Jedidiah spent in jail he was lucky just to keep from cleaning some asshole's clock.

Jedidiah held his breath as the district attorney strolled into the courtroom and took a seat at a table across from him. The prosecutor's name was Earl McKenzie. Earl was a towering man who stood taller than any man in the courtroom. A former college basketball standout, McKenzie could have played professional hoops if not for his love of the law. And he was good at law. McKenzie had put away more criminals in five years than his predecessor had in ten. Rumor was he was being groomed to run for the United States Senate. McKenzie came to court every day with two young assistants, a blonde bombshell and a young stud. It would not have surprised Jedidiah if the two aides could beat ole Henry in a trial without McKenzie's help.

It was the prosecutor's job to paint the worst possible picture of Jedidiah. McKenzie wasted no time slapping on the hate. In his opening remarks, McKenzie described Jedidiah as a misfit to society, a washed-up reporter, a writer without a conscious, and a liar out to slander the rich. McKenzie told the court how Jedidiah had been fired from the *Post* and unable to find work. The DA announced he had a long list of witnesses who claimed to see Jedidiah on the pier the night of the murder.

Jedidiah knew the witnesses were lying.

But why? Pawns of Libertore maybe?

And why were his coworkers going behind his back to discredit him?

The future senator brought it before the court that Jedidiah had made threats against the newspaper and its owners. This was partly true. Jedidiah had threatened to discredit them, not to do any physical injury.

In Henry's opening statement he informed the jury that Jedidiah was once nominated for the Will Rogers Humanitarian Writer of The Year Award. Other than Jacob Ross, Henry pointed out that Jedidiah was the most celebrated writer on *The Post* staff. There was no weapon recovered at the murder scene. Although he was in the habit of stumbling and tripping over his words, he did point out to the court the prosecution had no forensic evidence.

Getting fired was about the worst luck on Jedidiah. Without reporter credentials, none of the radio talk shows would listen to him. He tried to go on television with his Libertore theory but was rejected. Even being a guest on someone else's talk show was proving difficult to secure. Even friends cut him off, not wanting to be associated with a troublemaker.

Jedidiah took a sip from a bottle of water and set it back on the table. Carefully, he surveyed the jury. Juror six seemed to be outside of his element. The library-quiet courtroom appeared to make him nervous and jittery. Jedidiah could tell by the way he tapped his thighs with his fingers and bounced his knees, juror six would rather be in a noisy bar with a hundred television sets broadcasting every sport available.

"All rise for the court," sung out the bailiff.

Everyone in the courtroom stood to his or her feet as the squat, balding man made his way to the bench.

The Bailiff continued, "Hear ye, hear ye, the criminal court for the Fourth District is now in session. The Honorable Oswald Herbert Crane presiding. Let all who have matters come forth. May God bless this court."

After Judge Crane was seated, everyone in the gallery took his or her seat.

Judge Crane talked in a slow drawl that emitted from the deep back woods of Mississippi. Every time he opened his mouth, Jedidiah had clear visions of tall thick-limbed oak trees with ropes made of strong hemp formed into nooses, hanging off his every word. Judge Crane peeped out at Jedidiah over the top of his tiny-framed reading glasses. His sneer let Jedidiah know his future was sealed.

Jedidiah speculated if Crane was a member or not of Libertore. He scribbled the question on the backside of the dossier.

Juror ten was butt-ugly. Jedidiah hated to say that about anyone but he couldn't think of a nice way to describe her. The woman had to be at the bottom of the ugly barrel. That was no lie. She knew it herself because she never tried to make eye contact with the other jurors.

Jedidiah stared up at the spinning ceiling fans and imagined they were HH-46E search and rescue helicopters coming to airlift him away. This hostile courtroom wasn't that different than the desserts of Afghanistan. He'd spent six-months on a tour of duty over there, covering the war. Jedidiah shuffled his feet and repositioned his butt on the chair. This whole process was taking too long.

The old man in the big chair was having a go with his gavel and the loud banging brought Jedidiah down from the helicopter ride. Jedidiah covered his mouth as he suppressed a yawn. Something simple as a yawn might cause a jury member to think he was apathetic in his defense. He then clasped his hands atop of the desk and gave his full attention to the judge.

Chapter

Two

The phone rang, jarring Amber Lee from the dream she was having about being a high-priced call girl working the high-rise Vegas hotels. In her dream her clientele consisted of potbellied, middle-aged, married men with bank mortgages, kids with student loans, and bleached blonde wives addicted to country club alcohol. These underappreciated, at-home-lost-souls stood in line for her generous services. In her dream, Amber Lee always delivered as promised; her specialty was guaranteed to have them make repeat appointments. There was never an unsatisfied customer.

The phone rang again. This time Amber Lee opened one blurry eye and glared at it. Just maybe, if she pretended hard enough, the telephone would disappear and take whoever was on the other end away with it.

Damnit! She had to pee.

It was just as well for her to get up, answer the damn call, and then hit the toilet. The plan was a good one but to be truthful, she'd drank three Margaritas and two Manhattans last night at Duckworth's and she was still pretty wasted. Screw the phone, she needed to just go pee. Amber Lee wasn't down with being disturbed. After the eighth ring, the voice mail came on asking the caller to leave a message. This was followed by a gruff male voice filling the room.

"Damn it, Amber Lee. Pick up the fucking phone. I know your ass is home—I saw your car parked outside when I drove by five minutes ago. Quit being a bitch."

Quit Being A Bitch.

Those were just the words a woman wanted to wake up to.

Paul Jamison was a senior grade detective with the Robbery-Homicide Division of Third Street Precinct and very much married with two children with a third on the way. His wife Colleen was a high school math teacher and was devoted to her family. It was a shame she'd married such a loser. Three weeks into his relationship with Amber Lee, she discovered she'd been played and abruptly ended the affair with him. That was over a week ago, and the asshole continued to pursue her. It was getting to the point of harassment.

At first Paul was all apologetic—how sorry he was for misleading her—but he loved her so much he had to lie to be with her or his soul would've died. And to follow the bravado, he became the mighty swing dick on the block. What difference did it make that he was married, obviously, he could take care of business at home and with her. She had no complaints about the sex before she found out he was married, she should shut the hell up now. Paul pointed out that Amber Lee wanted the sex as much as he did, maybe even more since he had a wife at home to relieve some of his pressure. All Amber Lee had was a dildo.

Paul thought he was so cute with the corny lines. When none of his manipulations worked in having her come back to him, the pathetic begging started. He pleaded with her to come back and spend just one night for them to reconnect. This new phrase was creepy and bizarre. As an officer, Amber Lee only had to see Paul a few hours at work each day before they went out on assignments and even that was weird. She would look up from her paperwork and find him staring at her.

Amber Lee still felt the humiliation in her heart from that day she found out Paul was married. She was at The Gym, an athletic facility heavily frequented by off-duty police and fire personnel. Amber Lee worked out five days a week, usually early in the morning before the sun rose. One particular morning she failed to stick with her routine and dropped by The Gym just before noon. After working out a couple of hours she wrapped herself in a towel and took a seat in the corner of the sauna. It wasn't long before two male voices penetrated her calm surroundings. They were discussing her.

14

Amber Lee is the new meat and Paul Jamison always broke in the new meat first.

There was more said but she brushed the thought away. Amber Lee felt the whole dating scene was like a battlefield, complete with hidden land mines, machine gun fire, and overhead missile assaults. If on the off chance she found a suitable guy she'd like to spend time with, and maybe get close to, she had to be prepared that his preloaded baggage didn't have shit that disqualified her. The way she wore her hair, the scent of her perfume, a certain style of shoes, even a pair of damn earrings could trigger unpleasant memories and her date would be three sheets to the wind. Then she had to shuffle through the gay men and men who played on both teams.

Amber Lee's antenna usually picked up on married men a hundred yards away. In her loneliness, she'd let her guard down and Paul got in—into her heart, into her head, and into her cookies. The shame of being played made her angry enough to want to kill him, or at least chop his dick off. But in the end, she had no one to blame but herself. Paul didn't force her to spread her legs. His crime was being a charming liar.

Sometimes you could ask all the right questions, get all the right answers, make all the right moves, and still get played.

Sylvester bounded into the room and jumped up on the bed with her. The Chinese Shar-Pei was quiet and highly intelligent but a little stubborn when he wanted to be. Amber Lee thought it funny that all of her single girl friends had a dog or cat to keep them company. Women needed to have someone to talk to that wouldn't spread secrets or lies. Sylvester was Amber Lee's go-to and most trusted companion. And he knew to keep his mouth shut.

Amber Lee leaped off the bed and hustled to the bathroom. She squatted on the toilet without bothering to close the door. She watched Sylvester on the bed bury himself underneath the covers. Probably chasing after her sexual scent. Dreaming of being a Vegas call girl pretty much kept you moist between the thighs.

Chapter
Three

Jedidiah thought back to the first time he entered the Carver City Municipal Courthouse. Its gigantic size and high-domed ceiling had him awestruck. As a teenager, he couldn't help but be captivated and amazed by the marble floors, dark wood furniture, and polished brass stairs. Even as a youth he believed the atmosphere was gaudy and pretentious as if justice catered only to those who could afford it. In those days, anybody could wander about without much notice. Since 9/11, armed security was stationed at major check-points throughout the building.

The courthouse was divided into three wings—civil court, family court, and criminal court. At the entrance of each section were giant metal detectors and armed security guards. No one had a free pass, not even lawyers or secretarial staff could enter the courtrooms without being accurately search-ed. Only law enforcement and judges were allowed to carry weapons.

Before Jedidiah earned a journalism degree, he dreamt of being a lawyer. After seeing first-hand how lawyers lied to make a case, he suffocated the dream. Thoroughness and honesty was the journalistic integrity Jedidiah lived by. That commitment now seemed hollow to his ears. Ethics didn't mean a damn thing to rich people. It's what they taught the poor to keep them in line.

Jedidiah again gave focus on the jury pool. Juror one was a man with wide burly shoulders and a hang-dog expression forever etched on his face. Whenever he looked over at Jedidiah he did so with his head tilted down a little. His eyes would roll up to peer over his glasses like that of an old English professor.

Juror twelve was a woman of magnificent proportion packed into a smaller than normal body. Every time she wobbled into the courtroom, Jedidiah imagined her feet and knees screaming out in protest for the weight they endured. She even managed to wear a grin on her chubby face, happy just to be happy.

Sitting in his jail cell and in the courtroom, Jedidiah reflected often on the circumstances that got him locked up. He didn't like being ordered off a story. More importantly, he didn't like being told what information he could report. *The Carver City Post* owners chose what material was covered. Reporters were assigned stories by the news editor, Scott Kauffman.

Kauffman was middle-aged, of Jewish ancestry and well respected among the staff, except Jedidiah, who thought his boss was a sellout. Jedidiah knew about the free country club membership, the loaner cars from prestigious dealerships, skiing trips to Aspen, and unlimited air miles his boss received as kickback. Rich, powerful people and organizations got their confidential affairs swept under the rug all the time. It was no secret the Catholic Church was notorious for blocking stories. With their army of lawyers, and a legion of parishioners, the Catholic Church was virtually untouchable.

When Jedidiah didn't follow the status quo, his boss made sure there was a price to pay. The hell with the Scott Kauffman's of the world.

****

Without warning, the overhead lights went out. According to federal regulations, all public and government buildings were mandated to be equipped with battery powered backup lights in case of electrical failure. In this case, the emergency lights didn't switch on. In the darkness came the sounds of chairs being overturned followed by high-pitched screams. In the courtroom, there was chaos.

A sudden gunshot rang out.

Jedidiah witnessed the blistering flash not more than five yards away from him. A man's voice screamed out in anguish that he'd been hit. More shouts as people realized their lives were in danger.

Immediately, Jedidiah pushed back his chair and dove to the floor. He could feel his heart thumping violently inside his chest. His mind raced desperately out of control. Shouts and screams echoed throughout the darkness as more shots cracked the blackness. He heard others scrambling to get on the floor.

Jedidiah couldn't fathom something like this happening in an American courtroom. Yet, here it was. Courtrooms were conceived for civilized people who believed in unbiased justice for all. But impartiality was only as fair as the individuals selected to the jury. And each juror came wrapped in his or her own baggage and it only took one to nullify a whole jury. Jedidiah pressed his body to the floor thinking that dying was easy—It was living that was hell.

A few feet away, Henry Fowler was crying profusely for God to have mercy on his soul. Jedidiah whispered for him to keep quiet and not let the shooter know where he was. Unless, of course, the shooter was wearing night-vision goggles. Then it was game over.

Right now, the main thing was not to panic. Keep a clear head and think his way out of this mess. With no lighted exit signs to guide him, Jedidiah crawled in the direction he believed was the rear of the courtroom. If he could make it to the double doors and out into the hallway, maybe he would be safe.

The gunfire continued. It might have been eight or nine shots, Jedidiah couldn't tell for sure. Each shot made him recoil in fear. After gaining his nerve, Jedidiah slithered up the aisle.

Ka-boom! The blast was deafening. A burst of flames. Smoke and debris engulfed him. His ears filled with a continuous ringing. The noise switched to high-pitched screams.

Jedidiah's world went black.

****

Jedidiah lowered his head underneath the spray and smiled at how wonderful it felt. Jedidiah was without a doubt, the happiest man alive. Blessed with the perfect job, a spacious house, and the sexiest girlfriend alive, Jedidiah was truly blessed by God.

He heard the shower curtain being drawn back, and a moment later, the love of his life pressed against him in naked bliss. Jedidiah opened his eyes and was instantaneously overcome by the gorgeous beauty staring up at him. Light green eyes, full ruby lips, trimmed and arched brows, his lady was fine. Just minutes before, they had made love on the California king-sized mattress. The best part of waking up was having a goddess in his crib.

Last night they had a session outside in the rose garden under the full moon. Two young spirits, wild and free, dancing and prancing stark-naked under the stars. He could have at her morning, noon, and night and it would never be enough. Her body was a sumptuous feast and he responded with an insatiable appetite.

Her name was Erin.

"Will you have time for breakfast?"

"Only if I can nibble on your ear."

Erin gave Jedidiah an angelic smile and tilted up her chin. "I suppose that can be arranged. Right or left?"

"I'm famished. I'll have them both."

"Served right up."

Jedidiah lifted Erin up and took her against the shower wall. It was always like this with her—hot—wet—and wild. Erin squeezed his waist with her legs so tightly Jedidiah thought he was going to pass out. The agony and the ecstasy was pure and simple. Erin did things to him that no other woman before ever did. Jedidiah felt his release coming and he didn't deny it. He was depleted. They gyrated together for a while longer, absorbing each other's aura, communicating through tongues.

Later, as they were getting dressed for the day, Jedidiah playfully slapped Erin on the ass as she moved past him to the bedroom mirror.

"That's a breakfast I can have served all day, every day. With seconds."

"Whipped cream and strawberries next time," laughed Erin, giving him a wink. *"My treat."*

****

Jedidiah slowly opened his eyes. Cold water rained over him. Was he dreaming still? It took a moment to comprehend it was the overhead sprinkler system. The building must be on fire. He strained to get to his feet. His head felt like he'd been kicked by a mule.

The emergency lights were on now. Jedidiah couldn't believe the devastation around him. It was surreal. People were crawling on their hands and knees. Bloody bodies were sprawled on the floor and over benches. Those not dead were left dazed and confused, bleeding from the bomb fragments, crying loudly and sobbing softly. At the front of the courtroom, Judge Crane was slumped over his desk.

Jedidiah staggered to the front row and flopped down. His temple hurt on one side of his face. He reached up and touched the spot. Looking at his fingers, he was surprised to see they were smeared with blood. He wiped his hands on his shirt. To take his mind off his own injury, Jedidiah took inventory of the situation.

Up front the bailiff sat slumped against the wall. Obviously dead with his eyes still open. Juror five with the tattoos lay sprawled on the floor in front of the jury box sobbing. The Hispanic woman's entire upper body was drenched in blood. Gone was her gorgeous smile. Juror nine suffered a deep gash to the forehead that caused blood to stream down his narrow face. He sat in his chair staring straight ahead, in shock. Juror four rested her head back on the chair. Jedidiah could see the polite young woman was dead. Juror eleven lay on the floor next to the jury box bleeding profusely from a chest wound. His face was white as a sheet as he stared in a trance at the ceiling tiles. Juror seven could forget entering any future beauty contest. Her once lovely face was heavily scarred with deep cuts. Juror ten clung tightly to her arm as she moaned and rocked herself in her seat. To say she was butt-ugly before, she was double Dutch butt-ugly now. Juror eight wasn't going home tonight. It looked like a gunshot to the side of his head. Jedidiah quickly looked away.

Jedidiah caught a glimpse of Moose Dung, who was waving his hands excitedly and talking incoherently to Cockroach through cracked teeth and swollen lips. Moose Dung looked like he'd kissed a fast-moving Mack truck. Cockroach was covered with blood splatter and shaking badly, otherwise he seemed to be unhurt.

Above Jedidiah ceiling panels were missing, exposing electrical wires and broken water and sewage lines. The accumulation of heavy dust and smoke was making it hard for him to see and breathe.

More screams could be heard outside from the corridor. Turning back to the front of the courtroom, Jedidiah spotted the young female ADA being comforted on the floor by juror two and another man Jedidiah didn't recognize. The woman looked to be hyperventilating from fear. Lying next to her, on his side, was the second ADA, hemorrhaging from the back, probably a gunshot wound. McKenzie and the court steno-grapher were bent down over him. Jedidiah assumed that neither of them knew CPR. The two stared at St. James as if they expected Jesus Christ to come down from heaven at any time and lay healing hands on him. Yeah, good luck with that.

On the floor, a few yards away from Jedidiah, was his court appointed attorney, Fowler gulping for air like a fish out of water. It looked like a gunshot wound to the chest. He should have kept quiet. Jedidiah didn't see him making it to the hospital in time to save his life. For half a second, he thought of doing something to help the man but decided against it. He wasn't a doctor. He didn't have a first aid kit. There was nothing left to do but lie to the man that everything was going to be okay. Clearly it wasn't.

Juror six had nothing to be nervous and jittery about anymore. The man lay in the corridor face down not far from Jedidiah with blood pooling around his body.

Suddenly the rear doors crashed open. At once, the Special Weapons and Tactics team dressed in full body armor stormed into the room, shotguns drawn. Each member clothed in a black hood, tactical vest, and gloves. The S.W.A.T unit moved cautiously down the aisle using sweeping motions with their weapons to secure the room.

Jedidiah didn't dare move. Everyone is presumed guilty until proven innocent. It hadn't been determined as yet which one he was. Since he wasn't shot in the attack, it would be foolish of him to be shot in the rescue.

The person or persons responsible for this massacre was a professional. To get guns and bombs into the courthouse, they had to be working from the inside. What Jedidiah was looking at was a well-orchestrated hit.

But who was the real target?

To ensure safety, everyone who was physically able to walk was ordered to evacuate the premises. People shoved and pushed to get out. For a split second, Jedidiah thought about remaining seated, but then he was up and rushing out with the others.

In the corridor, three sheriff deputies were preoccupied, trying to keep the small crowd of onlookers from getting too close. Many of them had loved ones on the inside that they were worried about. A heavyset man dressed in a lime green first responder jacket waved for all the evacuees to follow behind him. Jedidiah stayed in step with the group until they turned the corner, headed toward what he knew was the cafeteria. Acting quickly, he bent over a water fountain and pretended to take a drink, thus allowing those behind him to pass. Sure no one was paying him special attention, Jedidiah exited the building and into the parking garage. Already a long line of cars and trucks were lined up to leave. Jedidiah was moved by the terror he saw on a young woman's face as her white knuckles gripped the steering wheel. The high-pitched wail of emergency sirens reminded him to keep moving with more urgency. Looking over the retention wall, Jedidiah could see a stream of bright red and blue lights coming in his direction.

The first place the police would look for him was with family and friends. He had to avoid all contact with everyone. Realizing that he would never get past the ticket gate operator without being challenged, Jedidiah took the emergency exit stairs down to the sidewalk. Rescue personal were steadily arriving on the scene. A section of the street next to the courthouse was curtained off with police cars to allow vehicles to exit the parking garage. In the chaos and confusion, Jedidiah vanished.

Chapter
Four

Amber Lee judged her reflection in the mirror. Her teeth were white and even, thanks to years of retainers and an expensive orthodontist. Lips just full enough not to be considered too thick. Her nose was just perfect for her face. Eyes appeared inquisitive, yet borderline nosy. Thank God, her eyebrows had room between them. Her hair long, dark and silky, thanks to Finesse shampoo. At five-feet-seven inches, she never tried to turn men's heads, but they turned anyway.

It was interesting that when she first came to Robbery-Homicide, especially after she started going out with Paul, all the male detectives found time to laugh and joke with her. Other than Amber Lee there were three other female detectives in the squad including her partner. The others, so far hadn't made any attempt to become acquainted with her.

Now that she had broken up with Paul, her male co-workers pretended to be too busy to grab a sandwich or go for drinks with her. It was for the better. Amber Lee didn't have anything good or worthwhile to say to them. For her to have slept with Paul was all in fun, a locker room prank so to speak, to them. She was an adult, no harm, no foul. He never forced himself on her but she wondered if the other female detectives had been seduced in playing Paul's little game. To ask them would be to pour gasoline over an open fire and she wasn't ready for the blowback. At least one of the ass clowns should have had the balls to speak out, especially her partner. The embarrassment of being played by a married man was not going to make her transfer. She was going to remain in the division and let all of them watch her rise up in the ranks. Amber Lee had graduated with high honors from the University of Phoenix with a Bachelor's degree in Criminal Justice. She'd finished at the top of the academy and passed the detective test her first try. She was an audacious mixed martial artist. No one could say she slept her way to success. But they would. Amber Lee knew they would. Unless she had a solid arrest record to prove otherwise.

Chapter

Five

When Jedidiah was a cub reporter, he'd covered a story about the homeless population in Carver City. He had been impressed by how they survived with so little. He was also taken aback by how invisible they were to the general public. Now Jacob Ross would be proud of how well he listened to his *on the run* stories. He was almost sure no one would look for him among the homeless.

Most of Carver City's transient population could be found on the Westend in the low-income neighborhoods of East Trade and Dunn. The Westend was a seedy district, popular with winos, junkies, crack-heads, gangbangers, drug dealers, and prostitutes. The locale was a good place for him to go off the grid as long as he kept away from ATM machines, convenience stores, and retail shops. Any business that dealt with the public would likely have surveillance cameras installed.

But first, Jedidiah had to take care of his head wound. At the corner of Dickson and Graham, he ducked into a Popeye's Chicken and turned immediately into the Men's toilet. Using paper towels, Jedidiah wiped the blood from his face and clothes. He was thankful the cut wasn't serious enough to require stitches.

It didn't take him more than fifteen minutes before he was out on the street again, bound for the Westend. Pedestrians passed Jedidiah in all shapes, sizes, and colors. From the very young to the very old—from the bored to the excited. A number of police vehicles rushed past Jedidiah in the direction of the courthouse. He was sure the authorities knew he was missing by now and an all-points bulletin had been issued for his arrest.

An hour after fleeing the courthouse, Jedidiah found himself strolling past tricks in search of a treat, partly dressed unshaven men hunched in doorways, some seated on steps, and several others leaning against retention walls. Most of the destitute appeared to be hopeless, godless, dreamless, and with no purpose other than to wake up. Their dull, lifeless expressions haunted Jedidiah as he shifted among them. Concerned as he was for his safety, Jedidiah understood he had to camouflage in their midst while he made his own investigation into the murder of Sal Hernandez. Undocumented workers went about their business every day without so much as a bleep on the radar. There was no reason a fugitive of the law couldn't do the same.

A panhandler with long yellowish fingernails and holding a battered old 'will work for food' sign hollered at Jedidiah as he hurried past. "Yo bruh, ya gotta smoke or sum loose change? I ain't ett in three days."

"Come with me. I got something better for you."

The man followed him into a nearby alley where Jedidiah talked him into exchanging clothes.

Jedidiah's first priority was to locate a safe place to sleep before the sun went down. Like an actor preparing to play a role, Jedidiah studied the street. Most transients slept underneath bridges, in tunnels, alleyways, and on park benches. Making her way slowly toward him was a poorly dressed woman pushing a shopping cart that contained all of her worldly possessions. He decided to follow her dumpster diving to see what locations she chose for survival supplies.

Chapter
Six

Amber Lee had not too long left The Gym when an alert came to her phone notifying her of the bombing at the courthouse. She immediately turned right at the intersection and sped in that direction. Traffic was backed up due to road construction so she turned on her blue flashing lights and maneuvered her way around it.

Once at the scene, she found herself in a madhouse of hysteria and confusion. Folks that weren't running were walking quickly away from the building. Amber Lee parked her car, exiting quickly, and raced over to a police officer standing behind a yellow tape, reading in bold block letters, 'Crime Scene Do Not Enter'. She flashed her badge and introduced herself as a detective before bending to duck under the tape.

The young officer wasn't having it. He held out his hand blocking her passage. "I'm sorry detective, but no one can get through until after the bomb squad and HAZMAT unit gives the okay."

Amber Lee sternly raised her voice. "But I need to be in there."

"And I need you to wait here."

"I have a job to do."

"So, let me do mine." He turned his face. "Please."

Amber Lee stood back and watched the commotion still going on outside. Black and gray smoke was filtering out a broken window on the third floor. The noise from emergency vehicles made it hard to hear. Amber Lee had to wait almost a half an hour for the Hazmat Unit to give the okay to go inside.

Upon entering, she noticed the courthouse was equipped with all the latest safety and surveillance equipment: high definition cameras, floodlights, motion sensors, metal detectors, and around-the-clock security. But yet somehow, weapons and explosives had been brought into the building.

The air was thick with the foul odor of smoke. The tile floor was slippery from the overhead water sprinklers. EMT personnel rushed past with a gurney transporting one of the injured to an area hospital. Never before had Amber Lee witnessed such a gruesome scene. There were blood pools everywhere. She pulled latex gloves from her pocket and slipped them on. The injured people, waiting to be transported, made painful moaning sounds that she couldn't tune out. Amber Lee counted fourteen corpses waiting for someone from the ME's office to come and pronounce them dead. Most of the expressions in the room she noted were of urgency and concern, or shock and disbelief. She wondered what her own face looked like.

Amber Lee tread carefully, all the while taking notes and shooting pictures with her Galaxy phone, trying to get a sense of what had taken place. From the looks of the burnt rubble, the bomb was detonated in the front section of the room.

"Sorry, I'm late," apologized Rosalind Kelly, rushing up to Amber Lee. "I had to take the kids to my mother's house." Rosalind pulled her thick black hair back and secured it with a ponytail holder.

Rosalind was tall for a woman, standing six-feet-three inches barefoot. When Rosalind was on the job she was all business. And she tried not to let police work interfere with her family life. She listened carefully while Amber Lee caught her up on what she'd seen and done so far. Three hours passed before they wrapped it up and headed back to Third Street.

Chapter
Seven

Jedidiah pushed his way in as close as he could to the volunteer workers distributing care boxes from the open backend of an eighteen-wheeler. Three hours on the streets and he already looked and smelt like he belonged. His newly acquired clothes were too small and his newly acquired shoes were too tight but he'd secured decent shelter.

A young Christian outreach worker on the street informed Jedidiah about giveaways at Saint Stevens. Photo ID was not required and the volunteers didn't make you sit and listen to a sermon about the goodness of God. Just show up at two o'clock, get a place in line, and receive your blessing.

After Jedidiah received his care box, he carried it to a clearing away from the parking lot. Making sure he wasn't followed, he sat cross-legged on the grass and opened the lid. Again, making sure he was not being stalked for his portions, Jedidiah poured the contents on the ground in front of him. A toothbrush, toothpaste, a comb, a bottle of water, a bar of soap, and a thin washcloth lay before him. There was an old saying, beggars can't be choosers, right? It was all stuff he could use and could not afford to buy. He picked up everything and placed it all back in the box.

It still pissed him off that he'd left the dossier behind in the fire. He needed the names and businesses of the old Libertore contacts to launch his own investigation. Without the folder, he had no way of knowing if any of the businesses were still in operation or if the owners were still alive or passed ownership to a family member. Without the file, he was basically screwed. If the dossier wasn't destroyed in the fire, it was in police custody. He thought about phoning the department and trying to find out who was assigned to the case. Upon weighing the consequences, he decided contacting the police for any reason wouldn't be in his best interest. He was an escaped convict with his face plastered all over the news.

Jedidiah began to put together a backup plan. The first place to start was with Sal. Find out why Sal was killed and by whom. The information on Libertore would take care of itself after that.

It was almost three o'clock and time for the day shift workers to end. The police would show up soon to harass the homeless off the street. When the suits got off at four it seemed like the police didn't want them to be bothered by those that didn't work. Jedidiah had witnessed earlier a couple guys get beaten for no other reason than they were broke and without a job. He scrambled to his feet and hurried to his private spot, keeping to the back alleys and less traveled streets.

Chapter
Eight

Amber Lee rushed into the briefing room and flopped down in the first empty chair she came to. She was near the back of the room but she could still see and hear the speaker.

Captain Samuel J. Pittman stood before the assembled task force with a grim expression upon his leathery face. He wore in his demeanor the collected years of responsibility as he approached retirement in six months. Pittman bent the mic down so he could address the men and women before him.

"Good afternoon, ladies and gentlemen. Thank you all for coming. Nothing like this bombing has ever happened in broad daylight in a courtroom. As you all know, we are in a war. Every day we come to work prepared to do battle with the same people we are sworn to protect. The media has our job under a high-powered microscope, magnifying every little detail of what we do, what we say, our reactions, and even our lack thereof. Some of the leaders in this city claim to have our backs, that is, until the heat gets too hot and the demonstrations take place in their front yards."

Pittman stared at the paper before him, reading, "An APB has been issued for Jedidiah Washington. At this time, he is not a person of interest in the bombing, but Washington is an escaped prisoner on a murder charge." He made eye contact with the men and women in blue again. "I've asked ATF, DEA, Homeland Security, and the SBI to join forces with us in identifying and apprehending our bomber. Working together, I'm positive we can get this situation cleared up quickly and efficiently. Thanks to all of you for your full attention to this matter. See your supervisors for further instructions." Without answering any questions Captain Hickman turned and exited the room.

Everyone began talking at once. Most of the officers seated around Amber Lee speculated the Dominicans were at the center. Like Hernandez, Montana and Gomez were both immigrants from the Dominican Republic. Since Sal Hernandez's death, Montana now ran the operations at Whale of a Fish Market on Clancy Street and Gomez was in charge of the fishing fleet.

Who did Montana and Gomez report to? Amber Lee wondered.

Chapter
Nine

The next day, Montana and Gomez were brought into Third Street Robbery-Homicide Division for questioning by the ADA, Broderick Gaines. Gaines was temporarily overseeing the case, while the lead Prosecutor recovered at home. Gaines was tall, slender with teeth as white as his hair and a mischievous twinkle in his eyes, but dangerously aggressive in his approach. Most people described being questioned by Gaines as likened to being fresh blood in the water with a shark. His thunderous voice had a way of intimidating folk into a confession.

Amber Lee, along with a dozen others on the task force, watched Gaines question the two racketeers on a wide screen television set up in the conference room.

Gaines entered the interrogation room and stood behind the two men seated at the small table on the opposite side with his back to the observation glass and live stream camera. "Glad you both were able to join me. This is not an official interrogation, or I'd be speaking to you separately. I just need to clear up a few rumors going around the city. Many of the investigators on this case think the bomb was put in the courtroom to kill both of you. Is someone not in agreement with the two of you running the Dominican cartel operation?"

Moose Dung Montana frowned at the ADA. He muttered through cracked teeth and swollen lips. "Desperate, nonsense talk. Tell me what *you* know, Big Man, so we both know, huh."

Gomez made it plain and clear that he didn't come downtown to rat on anyone by blowing off the question. "Tell me, what is your opinion of the fighting in the Middle East? Bad dudes over there," he chuckled.

Gaines continued but Amber Lee could tell he knew these two nuts weren't going to crack. "I think one or both of you know who bombed the courtroom?"

Montana waved his arms in disgust before folding them across his chest. "The hell you say?" He shifted indifferently away from the ADA.

Gomez laughed out loud while smacking the tabletop playfully. "I tell you what you should do; look for the guy behind on his child support payments. He's always the guilty suspect," he joked, looking up at the one-way mirror. He winked at the unseen people he suspected were watching on the other side.

It was obvious the two were no strangers to criminal proceedings. Montana and Gomez had an air of arrogance that rubbed Amber Lee the wrong way, as if they were indeed untouchable. Having Sal out of the picture they now had their own platoon of body guards following them around.

Gaines bent down and spread his big hands flat on the table. His voice became all business. "Why were you both in the courtroom on Monday? You were never present before."

Gomez shrugged noncommittally. "To see justice carried out just like everyone else."

Montana was more direct. "I thought your sister would be there."

Gaines stood straight and adjusted the sleeves of his freshly starched shirt. "Personally, I think it's too bad you're not down in the morgue."

Neither man looked directly at him. Gomez studied his own fingernails. Montana whistled a catchy tune.

Seeing he wasn't going to gain anything from the two, Gaines conceded. "If you hear anything on the street, I trust you'll let the department know. You're free to go."

Montana stood. "Stop pestering us. Leave it alone."

"I'll keep my ears open but don't hold your breath on me getting back with you, counselor," said Gomez leaving the room.

Amber Lee had a vivid vision of herself throwing mud pies at the goons and ruining their expensive tailored suits as they strutted through the precinct. A far cry from the casual attire they sported to the courtroom yesterday. From photographs she'd seen in evidence, the two had worn flowery shirts and were minus the chaperones.

What is really going on here? Amber Lee wondered as she watched Montana, Gomez, and the three bodyguards all crowd into one elevator.

Her intuition told her it was an inside job. Someone in leadership to get things done in the city had orchestrated the bombing. What she needed to establish was a clear and objective motive.

****

Later that evening Amber Lee ate supper at Zaxby's with her partner. She had the Cobb grilled chicken salad with Texas toast and bottled water. Rosalind had the four-finger chicken tenders with coleslaw, crinkle fries, Texas toast, and sweet tea. Zaxby's was a favorite to many in uniform for their half price appreciation discount.

"Who besides Washington, had the most to gain from the bombing?" asked Amber Lee, taking a bite of her salad.

Rosalind was eating her crinkle fries one at a time, deliberately dipping each one in the Zaxby's sauce before placing it in her mouth. "No one I can think of. Why do you ask?"

"Just checking over a few leads." Amber Lee took a bite from her Texas toast before asking another question. "If the trial had gone to completion, who stood to lose the most?"

Rosalind removed the plastic from the fork and dipped into her coleslaw. "I don't know. Someone who wanted Washington free. From what I hear he looked to be guilty as hell."

Amber Lee wagged her head reluctantly and took a drink from her bottled water. "So, how does the murder of Sal Hernandez fit into the bombing?"

"What makes you think Sal's murder and the bombing are connected?" asked Rosalind.

"That part is confusing. But if Jedidiah didn't kill Sal, as he insists, who did?"

"Another Dominican, maybe."

Amber Lee leaned closer to her partner so the man at the neighboring table couldn't overhear. It caught her eye that he was paying more attention to them than the woman seated across from him. "But why would they attack the courthouse? Why not the jail, or during prisoner transport?"

"You're assuming there is a reason for everything."

One key piece of evidence was a folder left behind on the defense table belonging to the defendant. It was a detailed description of the take down of Libertore Properties in the 1990s by a *Carver City Post* reporter named Jacob Ross. Jedidiah Washington was also a *Post* reporter. Amber Lee made a mental note to pay Ross a visit. On the back of the dossier, Jedidiah had scribbled a note to himself that Amber Lee found puzzling.

"Do you think Washington suspected Judge Crane of being a secret member of Libertore?" asked Amber Lee.

Rosalind was engrossed in one of those cable news programs where the host pretended to moderate the panel of talking heads in a current news story that everyone witnessed. Yet the narrative had to be reviewed, dissected, held up to a mirror, injected with artificial flavoring, then spread out in a format nobody could understand. After that argument to nowhere, they picked another topic of the day and began the whole process again. This is what passed for informative intelligent news today. No wonder everyone was confused over principles. After a minute, Rosalind turned to Amber Lee and shrugged. "Who knows."

Amber Lee tapped her fork nervously on the tabletop, thinking out loud. "Why would Washington suspect Crane?"

"Who cares." This time Rosalind didn't waste time looking around.

Amber Lee laid down her fork. The grilled chicken salad was delicious but she was too preoccupied to enjoy it. "Maybe Washington was working on a story."

Rosalind was getting short tempered. She turned to her partner. "Washington was fired from the Post. No one else would hire him. Let it go, why don't you, and finish your salad."

"Maybe it wasn't a mob or a Dominican attack, after all. Libertore just might still be in existence?"

Rosalind dropped the chicken tender she was holding and glared directly at her young partner. "I'm not interested in listening to you run your mouth while I'm trying to eat," she snapped, taking up a paper napkin and wiping her fingers. "I got kids at home for that shit. Our job is to collect the evidence, gather facts, conduct interviews, arrest the perpetrators, file said reports, and testify in court. It isn't in our pay grade to find any individual innocent or guilty. We bring in the perp for a jury to do that. Do you copy?"

Amber Lee looked away from her partner's frown. She was accustomed to eating her meals alone. Whether it be in front of the television, at the kitchen counter, or sitting on her bed, her freedom was unconstructed. "That still doesn't make me believe Washington had anything to do with the bombing." It was her theory that the opportunity presented itself for him to make an escape and he took it.

"If he was so innocent, why did he run? Now he's also guilty of escape and evasion."

Amber Lee didn't have an answer to that. Her whole notion was based on the dossier he'd left behind. The information in it was too important for her to just abandon haphazardly. Caught up in the confusion, he must've left it behind. Personally, she didn't believe in any of that Illuminati or Libertore boloney, but she'd seen enough in her thirty years of life to know anything was possible. It was also a possibility that the members of Libertore, if they existed, intended to silence Washington since his entire defense rested on exposing them. Amber Lee drew in a deep breath and composed herself. She had to be careful to keep a clear head and a sound mind. Once you started down the rabbit hole it was hard to think straight about anything.

"Look, I'm sorry I got on your nerves. Living alone I guess I didn't realize how important silence is for some people." Amber Lee eyed her partner.

Rosalind exhaled and resumed eating.

"Let's finish our supper."

Chapter
Ten

When he was sure that no one was paying any particular attention to him, Jedidiah crept over and retrieved a discarded newspaper from a tabletop adjacent to a coffee shop. He hid the paper underneath his clothes to avoid suspicion. A homeless man with interest in a current edition of the news might raise a few eyebrows. Jedidiah hurriedly made his way along the sidewalk until he reached the train station where he ducked behind a dumpster.

The front page of the morning paper carried pictures of the bombing. Jedidiah read the article by April Winehouse:

The bomb that exploded yesterday in the Criminal wing of the Carver City courthouse, killing fourteen people and sending nine others to area hospitals, is still without a motive. Police do not know if there is a connection with any known extremist groups. The DEA, ATF, SBI, and Homeland Security are working with the theory of a mob retaliation. Judge Crane is widely known for putting bad guys behind bars for a long time, often with no chance of parole.

The police still have no leads on where Jedidiah Washington is hiding or if he is still in the city. Washington was on trial for the murder of Salvador Hernandez when the bombing occurred.

The attack at the courthouse was the second largest bombing in the city's history. In June of 1995, thirty-nine people were killed and another sixty-three injured when a female assailant, acting under orders from a suspected crime syndicate, planted explosives at an evening church service.

The Fruit of Life Church was packed with worshippers along with high profile city leaders and media. After that bombing, the city suffered the worst rioting in its history.

Jedidiah tossed the paper into the dumpster. The article was all smoke and mirrors to Houdini the public. Winehouse was too lazy a reporter to do any serious research. A few phone calls, a couple of emails, and a Google search and she was ready to print.

According to the drug mules he'd spoken with on the street, that idea the mob was involved was bullshit. No crime family would expose themselves to that kind of high profile publicity. No street gang took credit, nor did the Dominican cartel. One thing was certain, the bombing was a well-executed operation and it went down without a hitch.

"Just like a military operation," Jedidiah whispered to himself.

"Look, there he is!" someone shouted.

When Jedidiah looked around, he realized he had been made. A portly man with dark glasses and a baseball cap, dressed in short canvas pants, and a green tee shirt was staring at him from across the boulevard. Before Jedidiah could look away, the man pointed at him and yelled.

"Hey you, don't move. Somebody call nine-one-one."

Jedidiah moved at once trying not to draw attention to himself. After a quick glance around, he saw the heavyset man was lumbering across the four-lane street toward him. Jedidiah turned quickly into a parking garage and headed straight across, in hope to exit on the other side. He was halfway when he heard a commotion coming from behind. Not daring to look around, he zigzagged his way across, keeping lower than the parked vehicles. When the shouts grew louder Jedidiah crawled beneath an SUV. A minute later he watched the soles of three men trot past where he was hiding. Without waiting for them to circle back, he scrambled from beneath the SUV and made a quick hustle over to the stairwell. Taking two steps at a time, he bounded up to the first floor. Jedidiah found himself in a small lobby facing a line of shops.

Before going out on the busy street, he pulled his ball cap down over his eyes. None of the midmorning shoppers paid any attention to him. Jedidiah trotted briskly past the clothing shops and chain eateries until he arrived at Hudson

42

Boulevard. He crossed Hudson and hurried up the block in the opposite direction of where he stayed. He didn't want the street cameras to give away the directions to his safe place. A total of three police cruisers screamed past him, headed in the direction of the parking garage. Out of breath and shaking with fear, Jedidiah finally stopped six blocks away from the train station at a hot dog stand. He sat down at a table out of sight to evaluate his predicament.

Chapter Eleven

It was obvious to Amber Lee she would need to continue to run her own independent investigation without her partner. She discovered from court records that Salvador Alfred Hernandez had been arrested twenty-six times: only one conviction for a small-time robbery over twenty years ago. He appeared before Judge Crane three times over the last five years. Each time his case was dismissed for lack of evidence or failure of a key witness to appear to testify against him. Earning him the nickname El Fuego Del Diablo on the street.

Judge Crane had a reputation for being tough on mobsters. If he wasn't in collusion with Libertore why didn't he recuse himself from Sal's cases? Amber Lee wondered. *Sal always beat the evidence when Crane presided. Did this mean the judge pool was corrupt? That would mean political corruption.*

She didn't think the Dominicans would have sanctioned the attack with two of their bosses in the courtroom. Fearing she'd come to a dead end, Amber Lee needed to bounce her ideas off someone other than Rosalind and the other detectives. Kaleah Stevenson and Mercedes Marshall still weren't acknowledging her. Gathering all her notes and files, Amber Lee went to Captain Pittman to get his opinion. He listened while she brought him up to speed on all she had uncovered, including the ties to Libertore.

When she had laid out all the facts before him her Captain spoke up, "I commend your effort, but right now we have a suspected killer on the loose and we have an unexplained bombing with fourteen dead. For all we know, the bombing could have been orchestrated by a rival cartel making moves on Sal's territory," Captain Pittman suggested. He turned back to his computer. "In any case, you need to focus your time and energy on bringing Washington in." Pittman slipped a pair of reading glasses on and leaned in closer to the computer screen.

Amber Lee didn't follow that theory for a minute. She also caught the subtle hint that the conversation was over as far as her captain was concerned. Not giving up easily, she said, "If that were the case, wouldn't the confrontation have taken place in Sal's district?"

Captain Pittman turned back to Amber Lee. He answered her question with a question of his own, "So, who do you think we should be looking for?"

Amber Lee shrugged. "Members of Libertore."

"Quite frankly, they don't exist."

"Jacob Ross and Jedidiah Washington believe they do. They put together a dossier on them."

Pittman frowned. "Maybe you should just stick with the investigation already at hand." He picked up a clipboard with notes attached to it and tossed it over to her. "Reports are coming in from all over town of Washington sightings. That should keep you busy." He went back to his work, rolling his chair closer to the desk. "Close the door on your way out."

There. She was officially dismissed. Amber Lee went back to her desk disappointed. *Why was she so interested in clearing Washington?* She asked herself. *What did she really know about him?* She picked up her file on Washington and read.

The closest person she'd been able to find in Jedidiah Washington's life had been a woman named Erin Snow. Erin Jane Snow was a professional photographer, killed along with sixty-two other passengers in a Boeing 737-800 plane crash in March of 2016. Erin was a freelancer for major magazines and newspapers, with her work highly sought after. Erin and Jedidiah had been engaged but she died two months too soon.

Amber Lee put down Washington's file and picked up the file on Sal Hernandez.

One of the detectives supposedly killed and butchered by El Fuego Del Diablo was James Dubach. The two met at the academy. Amber Lee remembered Dubach as a smooth talker, fine-ass dresser, a little over the top with attitude, anxious to make his way up the ladder. He viewed undercover work as a sure chance to promotion. Less than two months after getting a job on the docks, he ended up dead.

Amber Lee tossed the file on top of Washington's and sat back in her swivel chair, staring up at the ceiling. The more she learned, the more she found out she didn't know. There were too many unanswered questions. *Why did the security cameras go black in the hallways just before the attack? Who all had access to the control room?*

Her thoughts were interrupted when her partner entered in the squad room engaged in agitated conversation with Captain Pittman. They stood near the door with their backs to Amber Lee for over ten minutes. Finally, Pittman patted Rosalind on the shoulder before turning and leaving.

When Rosalind sat at her desk Amber Lee turned to her and asked, "Were you talking about me? I'm a big girl. You can tell me."

"No, we weren't. We were talking about the task force progress. Something you don't seem to be interested in," Rosalind added.

"I'm interested. I think the bomber had to have inside help with the cameras and the lights. I think we should talk to the County Supervisor and find out who was working Monday."

"Good idea, Rookie. Glad to have you back working with the rest of us."

****

Amber Lee arrived at The Gym just after five-thirty A.M. She did her usual routine of squats, bench presses, curls, treadmill, and lunges. This was followed by intense sessions of judo and kickboxing. It was near eight o'clock when she showered and dressed. Her mood was good because she'd slept straight through the night before and was looking forward to speaking with the county supervisor. She was also starving. Three scrambled eggs and fresh kale topped with a slice of provolone cheese sounded tasty.

As Amber Lee neared her car, the hair on her neck stood on end. The granite-colored Dodge Charger was where she'd left it but the doors were standing open. She immediately drew her Glock 19 and cautiously advanced, careful of the other cars in the parking garage. Someone could still be hiding—watching—waiting to attack her. Adrenaline level high, heart pumping a mile a minute, Amber Lee moved closer. Peeking inside the Charger, she eyed the opened glove compartment. Her registration and insurance papers were scattered on the floorboard. The brown satchel she'd left on the front seat was missing. The satchel contained the file that belonged to Washington. She did a complete search of the interior. The only thing she could find missing was the satchel.

Amber Lee immediately took out her cell and phoned Rosalind. Her partner answered on the second ring. "My car was broken into this morning. The only thing the perp took was Washington's folder."

"Are you sure?" Rosalind sounded preoccupied.

Amber Lee could hear kids laughing and playing in the background.

"Are you back on that Libertore kick. You're as bad as Washington."

"Okay, if Libertore doesn't exist, why did the perp take only that folder?"

"Stop being paranoid. I'll meet you at Third Street in half an hour." Rosalind disconnected the call.

Amber Lee did a quick visual check of the parking area before she called for a patrol car. While she waited, she thought about who knew she had the folder: her captain, of course, and her partner.

It took less than five minutes before Officer Cash arrived and took down Amber Lee's statement. After Cash left, she got in her Charger and pointed it in the direction of Third Street. The day no longer looked so optimistic.

Chapter
Twelve

Jedidiah opened his eyes. Immediately, his muscles tensed as sudden fear gripped at his insides. A vision flashed of him narrowly escaping being caught the day before. He watched the police comb through the downtown streets but come up empty. He was certain they would increase their presence in the Westend.

Around him, darkness, except for the light visible from distant high-rise windows. Slowly the realization of his existence crept back to him. He remembered he wasn't back at his apartment, nor was he in the city lock-up, but a man on the run living on the street. Jedidiah sat up then and tucked his legs beneath him, shivering at the cool early morning air. *He was wanted on a capital murder charge.*

The neighborhood he chose to hide in had congested traffic, crowded sidewalks, multiple tourist traps, gift shops, a pan-cake house, a smoke shop, and a convention center. He'd found a safe enough place to sleep on the roof of a boarded-up photo shop. Out of old cardboard, he'd made a makeshift bed behind a furnace duct. Nothing to bother him up here but a few pigeons and an occasional bat, which he admitted, scared the piss out of him. On the backside of the abandoned building was a rickety fire escape ladder, leading up to the top of the two-story building. This, he used to go down in the early morning and up late at night.

Directly behind the photo shop was an Asian-ran dry cleaners that didn't close until after nine in the evening. Jedidiah had to wait until all the employees left for the night before venturing up the fire escape. The dry-cleaners had a security light mounted to its rear. It cast a dim yellow glow that was almost useless to see by. Still, Jedidiah was careful not to be seen. As yet, he hadn't seen a security guard but thinking rational, there had to be one assigned to the area.

Chapter Thirteen

The Embraer Legacy 600 cruised at a speed of 500 mph, high above the ground, carrying seven passengers and a crew of three on a transatlantic flight. The private business jet was built in Brazil at a cost of twenty-six million dollars. After serving chardonnay, and a first-class meal of roasted chicken breast, braised cannellini beans, Chanterelles, and lemon confit for dessert, the female assistant disappeared into the cabin to join the captain and the co-pilot. Now was an opportunity for business to be discussed—a time for decisions to be made. Lives would be changed. Money possibly made. These men influenced authority. To say they existed as a group would be hard to prove because no camera ever captured them all together in one place. This was possible by secret airfields, private limousines, and a staff sworn to secrecy with the penalty of death.

Tucker McCorkle had a lot on his mind this afternoon and it had nothing to do with the remote airfield he operated. He shared with the five men seated around him what he was thinking as he cut into his roasted chicken breast. "I agree that actions were needed to sanitize Sal. He was getting too big for his britches. But at what point do we say enough is enough?"

Another member answered, "Frankly, I never liked the slimy bastard. Good riddance to bad garbage." He gave a toast in the air with his wine glass.

McCorkle continued, "I'm concerned that the sanctions enforced against Washington and Judge Crane has opened us up to tremendous scrutiny. Some hot-shot with a badge might go poking around, stirring up trouble." He took a bite and smiled his approval of the dinner.

Carl Madison, in a calm voice, responded between chews. "We've faced Dirty Harry types before. We have people to back them down." Madison managed some hedge fund worth millions.

"Or grind them into shark bait," chuckled a member seated a few feet away from Madison.

Everyone squirmed at the idea of being chopped into shark food. The image of severed bodies ruined several appetites.

The elderly gentleman seated next to the jokester turned irritably at him and barked, "It's that kind of arrogance we can certainly do without," condemned the chairman of the board at Amtric Ammunitions.

McCorkle concurred, "I agree. We need to continue to work within the brotherhood. What Sal did with those two detectives was gross negligence."

The chiseled-faced Native American knew how to get away with murder. It was how he made his living. His name was *Bhoot.* The Indian word for ghost. He laid down his fork. "What do you all suggest we do about the girl detective?" He looked around the cabin at his peers while he waited for a response. "She's determined to find out what Washington was looking into. I'm told she's bright—asking all the right questions."

"We have the dossier back and it's been destroyed," pointed out the jokester. He wanted nothing else to do with murder. "There's nothing further we need to do." It didn't appear that was the answer Bhoot was waiting for.

"If I could make a suggestion," said a man with stained, capped teeth.

Bhoot was an international real estate broker. He knew there were other methods to dispose of dead bodies. A concrete grave, maybe. "Go ahead," he said.

Capped Teeth lit a cigarette. His eyes seemed to be seeing the faces of the two deceased officers. His tone was serious, "Arrange a break-in at Jacob Ross's home and find whatever computer files he may have saved on Libertore. After that, I say we scare the girl off. Don't kill her but make her wish she was dead."

There was silence for a moment.

Bhoot smiled, "That's a better idea."

"The police still haven't picked up Washington," said the corporate lawyer turned politician. This man had been elected to the House of Representatives eleven years ago. He was currently up for re-election. Polls gave him a four percent margin over his opponent. "He needs to be eliminated. Right now, the alphabet agencies suspect Crane was the target. Good heavens, we don't need a retrial."

"I'll have my people get right on it," said Bhoot.

Chapter
Fourteen

A large dark-colored SUV pulled up next to Amber Lee on the freeway. Out of the corner of her eye, she noticed the passenger side window slide down. Glancing over, she found herself staring at the muzzle of a Berretta M9. Immediately, she slammed on the brakes and steered to her right, causing the Charger to spin in a circle. When she recovered, she saw the SUV had spun around also and was coming back.

"What in the hell?"

Amber Lee stepped on the gas pedal and raced away, weaving in and out of oncoming vehicles. Her heart almost stopped when she saw two tractor-trailers coming straight toward her. Acting quickly, Amber Lee cut to her left, scraping the guardrail, barely avoiding being crushed.

"Damnit, damnit to hell!"

The car bounced around like the silver ball in a pinball machine.

With the SUV in hot pursuit, Amber Lee sped to the nearest oncoming ramp and drove up the grade, against traffic. Cars came at her with their horns blaring and head-lights flashing. She was barely aware of the angry glares as she flew past. At the top of the road she veered into the traffic stream.

Where was the highway patrol when you needed them?

Glancing in her rearview mirror, the SUV was still behind her and closing ground.

"Who the hell are you guys?" she screamed in terror. Her heart sank when she saw her cell phone fly off the passenger seat and onto the floorboard. Turning the wheel sharply to avoid a slow-moving minivan caused the cell phone to disappear underneath the seat.

"Damnit to hell."

Moments later, Amber Lee reached the intersection of Ross and Green to find stalled traffic. She couldn't go any further. Without bothering to retrieve her cellphone, Amber Lee leaped from her car and climbed over the cement barrier. She had her service weapon on her. If she could find shelter she'd risk having a shootout.

Amber Lee continued to sprint down the crowded sidewalk past gift shops, a pancake shop, and a convention center. Surprised patrons jumped out of her way as she yelled aloud for someone to call 9-1-1.

Three blocks later, Amber Lee cut down an alley between a smoke shop and an abandoned photo shop. She found herself in a small space, staring at the rear of a dry cleaner. It was a dead end. Turning around, she noticed a fire ladder lowered within her reach. Like something out of a James Bond movie, Amber Lee jumped and grabbed ahold. She climbed rapidly to the rooftop. Making sure she wasn't followed, she pulled up the ladder and crouched behind the wall. She took out her Glock and whispered a prayer.

Amber Lee heard the rattle of the ladder being pulled down. It was after ten o'clock P.M. and the dry-cleaners had closed. Whoever the homeless person was whose belongings she'd found, was returning for the night. She held her Glock and waited.

Chapter
Fifteen

After the news hit the street that a woman abandoned her car on the freeway and was last seen in the Westend District, Jedidiah decided to flee the area until dark. Years ago he'd written an article on the poor in Carver City when he learned of an underground railroad. An unmarked truck would pull up at a certain stop and those who felt the need to get away for a while, climbed inside. No questions asked. The truck would drive along a secret route to a mysterious location. When fugitives were ready, a truck brought them back. Again, no questions asked. Unlike metro transit, there was no posted schedule.

"All right, hold it right there. What the hell are you doing up here?"

Jedidiah froze. He could barely make out from the dim light a young woman dressed in workout clothes. In her hand was a gun pointing at his chest. "I live here. What are you doing up here?"

"I'm Detective Amber Lee of Third Street Precinct Robbery-Homicide Division."

Jedidiah slowly turned to go back down the ladder.

"Wait! Hold it right there." She recognized him. "Get your hands up. Now! Do it!"

Jedidiah raised his hands over his head. It was over. Just like that. He was captured before he could find out anything to justify his escape. Yet, the events of the day prompted him to ask, "Are you the woman the police are searching for?"

"Yes."

"Word on the street, you're a police officer wanted for questioning," Jedidiah attempted to switch the focus on to her.

"Me? Why?"

"You're a dirty cop. I heard rumors of everything from murder to armed robbery."

"You're lying. Someone is trying to frame me."

"Yeah. That's what I said."

"Only I'm telling the truth."

"Just like that, I'm a liar," Jedidiah smirked.

"You were arrested and on trial."

"If your buddies would've caught you this morning, you'd be on trial."

"That wasn't the police chasing me."

"Then who was it?"

"I've been asking a lot of questions about Libertore."

"Libertore?" Jedidiah repeated. He was puzzled by her interest.

Nearby, a bat took flight starling them both. Amber Lee flinched as Jedidiah ducked his head. A look of mutual agreement passed between them.

Amber Lee lowered the Glock. "I found the dossier you left behind. I think we need to talk."

****

"Why'd you run?" asked Amber Lee, the service weapon beside her, in easy reach if Washington made a move toward her. So far, he showed no signs of trying to run.

Now that he could see her better, Jedidiah thought she was more beautiful than a body had a right to be. Still, she was a cop and had a loaded gun. "I didn't murder, nor did I have anything to do with the murder of Hernandez," responded Jedidiah.

They sat five feet apart on the rooftop. The city skyline was colorful tonight. "The first gunshot was only a few yards from me. I took cover on the floor. I suspect my attorney Henry Fowler got the bullet meant for me. The bomb was planted near the defense table. By the time it detonated, I was already on the floor crawling towards the rear exit. I admit I was wrong for leaving the scene. But I was, and still am, in fear for my life. I'm being framed for a crime I didn't commit. I don't trust the police to protect me because I think they're the ones trying to kill me."

"This may come as a shock to you but I think the police are trying to kill me as well. I only told two people about your folder. No one else knew I was investigating a Libertore angle. And the gun pointed at me from the SUV was police issued. A Berretta M9."

"Like it or not, we have something in common."

"Why'd you have a public defender in the first place? You made a decent salary at *The Post*."

Jedidiah shook his head and looked up at the sky. "I've been laid off nearly a year. My savings was used up. By the time I was charged with murder, I was broke. I knew that public defenders were overworked, underpaid, and had no relationship with their clients. They can barely even put a face with a name. Eighty percent of their clients are found guilty whether they are or not."

"Since most clients can't afford bond, they lose their jobs."

"Liberty and justice for all is a freaking joke. No money will guarantee you a job upstate making license plates."

"Unfair, I know. I don't sentence suspects I just bring them in."

"How much concern did you feel for the homeless before now?"

"I can't say I really paid that much attention. Some of them, I'm sure, could have made better choices with their lives."

"A lot of hookers started out as beautiful young women before the streets beat them down. Don't get it twisted," Jed corrected.

"I'm sorry, I suppose I didn't care. I didn't notice," Amber Lee conceded.

"That's how I can hide in plain sight."

They sat in silence for a minute. Both taking in what the other said. An emergency siren split the night air, piercing at first, and then slowly retreating.

Finally, Jedidiah asked, "So, what do we do now?"

"I could take you in but that wouldn't solve our problem. You'd die in jail and I'd meet up with another unfortunate accident."

Jedidiah changed the subject. "How long have you been a detective?"

"Not that long. This is my first major case."

"Oh, really. Damn."

"Hey look, I helped solve a few high-profile B & E's."

"That's a far stretch from murder."

"Yeah, well."

"What did you do to piss off your *Blue Brotherhood?*"

Amber Lee blew air out of her cheeks. "Sometimes a cop who refuses to be corrupted doesn't fare so well. They can't be trusted. I guess that's how they see me. Not loyal to the code."

It was good for Jedidiah to have someone to talk to. First, he taught Amber Lee how to change her appearance and to keep a low profile while out in the public. Then he coached her on down playing her inquisitive cop's instinct. Homeless people didn't seek to find answers that weren't in front of them. A vacant stare was more believing than a keen glance. Amber Lee had to pretend a part of her soul was dead on the inside. And then there were the basic rules of the street. Waste not, want not and one man's trash was another man's treasure.

Chapter
Sixteen

It was after five P.M. and Centre Towers was nearly de-
serted. The few workers lingering after business hours were
the cleaning crew, building security, and a few over-timers.
Having worked in the building for almost eleven years,
Jedidiah knew their routine. Towers Busy Brooms started on
the twentieth floor and worked their way back down to the
front entrance. Zenith Security guards walked each of the
twenty floors checking to make sure the doors that were
supposed to be locked, were indeed locked. The over-timers
could be found at his or her desk. Floor to ceiling windows
wrapped the building, showcasing the magnificent and
breathtaking city skyline.

The *Carver City Post* business offices were located on
floors six, seven, and eight. The sixth-floor consisted of three
conference rooms, a training room, and a meeting room. The
seventh-floor housed the advertising offices and a break room
with ten sixty-inch widescreen televisions. Today's news was
updated minute-by-minute and around the world updates
were a necessity. The eighth-floor was where the reporters did
their work in digital format. The majority of readers used a
phone, tablet, or a desktop computer to read the news.

Editor Kauffman often worked late but not finding him in
his office on the eighth floor, Jedidiah headed down to the
seventh-floor break room. He used the stairs to avoid being
seen in the halls. He was about to step out of the stairwell
when a sales executive came out of the break room, headed
to the elevator. After she entered and the doors shut, Jedidiah

headed quickly to the break room where he could see Kauffman through the glass door standing at the counter. He was alone. Jedidiah flung open the door as the editor was pouring a cup of coffee. The sudden intrusion startled Kauffman, causing him to drop the coffee pot. The glass carafe crashed into pieces onto the floor, coffee splattered onto the cabinet doors and Kauffman's pants and shoes.

"Dammit!"

"How much did they pay you to set me up?" hissed Jedidiah, without an introduction.

Kauffman's eyebrows raised. "They who? Set you up for what? What are you talking about? How'd you get in here?"

Jedidiah marched up to his former boss with a white box tucked under his arm. He had to hurry before someone interrupted them. "Libertore is responsible for the bombing. But you know that. I was supposed to take the fall."

Kauffman snatched a paper towel from the dispenser and swiped at the coffee stains in his clothes. "Libertore does not exist."

Jedidiah set the box he'd been holding down on the counter top. "I have here a bomb. Unless you tell me what I want to know, I swear, I'll detonate it."

Kauffman backed away a few steps. His back was against the wall. He had no idea what Jedidiah knew about bomb making. His eyes darted frantically for an escape route. He looked sick when he realized there was nowhere to run.

"Are you shitting me? I told you I don't know anything. Get that damn thing outta here."

"I think you're lying. In fact, I know you're lying."

"Wait!" Kauffman threw up both hands. The years in the news business had scarred his memory. Horrific images of scattered body parts after a bombing were not easily forgotten. "There was a guy last year—I forget his name—said if I fired you, his firm would flood the paper in advertisements. So, I did."

"Did he say why he wanted me fired?"

"I didn't ask. Sales were down. Reducing staff and getting a new client in one throw. It was a no brainer." Kauffman loosened his tie and undid the top two buttons on his sweat-soiled shirt. He looked to have a seizure at any minute.

"What was his name?"

"What?"

Harvey Butaloon Degree Sr.

"You heard me."

"He represented a major advertising firm. Said he was the company president."

Jedidiah picked up the empty box and hastily retreated.

Chapter
Seventeen

Captain Pittman was dining alone at Gertrude's Restaurant seated in front of a gigantic bay window, overlooking a beautiful courtyard, decorated with leafy plants. Begonia luxurians, crown shaft palms, caladiums, canna, coleus, and Hosta decorated his view. His meal of Tomahawk ribeye, rubbed in smoked salt was expensive, and in his opinion, worth every nickel. Gertrude's was his favorite hideaway from the public's damn demands. Pittman looked up and was surprised to see one of his detectives being escorted to his table.

Amber Lee lied to the maître d' that she was Pittman's guest. She sat at the table, across from her Captain. She'd cleaned herself up to enter the restaurant, that way he couldn't associate her with the homeless population.

"Will you be dining, ma'am?" asked the maître d'.

"Nothing for now. Maybe coffee later," she lied.

The maître d' left them alone.

Amber Lee casually placed her Glock on the table, underneath a cloth napkin, so only her boss could see it.

Pittman's eyes grew wide as saucers. He laid aside his knife and fork.

"What do you want?"

"Glad to see you, too."

"All right. What is it you want?"

"You conspired to have me killed."

"That's the most ridiculous accusation I've ever heard."

Amber Lee could see the sweat beading on his forehead and could hear his labored breath.

"Explain to me how the day after I confided in you, two goons in a dark SUV forced me off the freeway. I don't see that as a coincidence."

Pittman stuttered. "I don't see it as anything else. It could be entirely related to another case you're working on."

"I may be a new detective but I'm not naive."

"No one implied that you were." Pittman gave Amber Lee an icy stare. "I'm just saying you should look at all the facts thoroughly before you go making false conclusions."

"I have."

"By the way, we rescued your dog and put him in a shelter."

"That was mighty decent of the department. I appreciate it."

"We're not the bad guys here, Amber Lee. You should know that."

"I act on what I see. Getting back to the subject at hand, who authorized the hit on me?"

"Detective, I can have your badge for such gross insubordination," said Pittman through gritted teeth.

Amber Lee shrugged. "You can have my badge. Give me a name or I make a scene right here and now."

Pittman frowned. "I've got nothing more to say to you."

Amber Lee uncovered the Glock to show she wasn't bluffing. A large woman with burgundy color streaks in her hair sitting alone at the adjoining table noticed the weapon and sprang to her feet. The frightened diner stopped a hostess and pointed back at Amber Lee.

"You don't have a lot of time before police cruisers pull up outside. At that time, we both get chalked."

Pittman glanced down at the gun, and then lifted his eyes back to Amber Lee. He was too close to retirement to play hero. Given time, some problems had a way of taking care of themselves. "Richard Popson. He's CEO at Amtric Ammunitions. Talk to him. I saw him talking to Rosalind Monday night outside the courthouse."

Saying her partner's name caught Amber Lee by surprise. "Rosalind? What were they talking about?"

Amber Lee could see the hostess now talking excitedly to a woman who might have been the manager. They both had their eyes on her. A few other patrons were becoming curious.

"How the hell should I know? I asked the next day and she wouldn't say."

"Thank you. Enjoy the rest of your meal." Amber Lee sprang to her feet and made a hasty exit through the kitchen and out the rear of the building.

Chapter
Eighteen

An investigative reporter's job might seem to be glamorous to a novice observer, but it wasn't. For starters, you had to have dependable, reliable sources. Getting someone to open up when the consequences of his or her actions was not in their favor, and in some instances, harmful, wasn't an easy order. A snitch, stool pigeon, narc, or whatever you labeled the blabbermouth, could pay heavily for sharing secretive information. Writing a story on suspicious evidence could land the reporter in legal jeopardy or fired.

A major news outlet recently released three award-winning journalists for not following proper protocol when substantiating a story. First, a story had to pass the fact checkers, and then adhere to journalism standards before given to experts and lawyers to solidify the details. When a reporter refused to give up his or her source in court, they sometimes found themselves behind bars in contempt. If the information was too hot and the person of interest had much to lose, the reporter might be threatened or killed. The leaker would know then the fate that awaited him or her.

Jedidiah knew all this when he signed up for the job. The sense of doing the honest and right thing had always been at the center of whom he was and how he tried to live. He had committed himself too deeply with Libertore to back down. Exposing the secret organization was his only option.

"This is what we do know," Jedidiah said to Amber Lee back on the rooftop. "Kauffman pitched me off to Lynch Advertising. This guy Lynch supposedly paid him for massive amounts of ad space to fire me in exchange. Kauffman swears there was no direct reason given."

"Pittman told me about my partner talking to a guy named Popson, president of Amtric Ammunitions, outside the courthouse the night of the bombing."

Jedidiah frowned. "Seems like I remember the names Lynch and Popson from the Libertore dossier."

Amber Lee took a bite from the Gala apple she'd liberated from a fruit stand on the corner the night before. "I wonder what Rosalind is doing with someone connected to Libertore?"

Jedidiah shrugged. "Money. Maybe they paid for her loyalty."

"She never talked about finances or shared a lot about her private life."

"Sal was killed a month after the two detectives were murdered, which leads me to suspect his death was in retaliation. Therefore, we could have a rogue cop on our hands."

Now Amber Lee shrugged. "Yeah, but why frame you? And why come after me?"

"Libertore is the only connection."

"You believe Libertore plays both sides of the law. That can only mean high-level police corruption. Your thinking is a bit extreme."

"You have a better theory?" Jedidiah searched her face.

"Not at the moment. Those undercover detectives Sal had killed were James Dubach and Dan Cunningham. If I could get online, I could look into their backgrounds. Find out who they were close to on the force. What I would give to have my cell phone about now."

"Cell phones can be tracked with GPS. You're better off without it. There's a Holiday Inn not far from here. They have public computers for their guests. In all the years I stayed with them I've never been approached. I can take you there."

"You pretty much have this street life figured out."

"I did a piece on the homeless a few years back. I made connections."

****

To be falsely accused of doing something you know you didn't do had a way of humbling the proudest of people. Jedidiah noticed that Amber Lee no longer made a motion for her gun when he got close to her. Two nights in a row she slept soundly, assured in the fact he wasn't going to attack or abandon her. He felt the trust was mutual. She was pretty like Erin. Smart like Erin. But, of course, she wasn't Erin.

Erin was dead.

His constant dreams weren't going to bring her back. No number of tears would awaken the sound of her singing voice. It was ironic he'd find himself so close to such a beautiful, intelligent woman like Amber Lee at a time when he had nothing. She was in his element now. She needed and depended upon him and his street smarts was all he had to offer her. After it was over, then what? He laid his head down and slept.

Chapter
Nineteen

Amber Lee looked up and was surprised to see Rosalind and her ex-lover, Paul Jamison on Canal Street. She watched as they stopped at several merchants, showing them photos. In an instant, she understood they were canvassing the neighborhood. Surely there were others in the area. She was right.

Directly across the street, Detectives Stevenson and Marshall were speaking with a young Asian woman who sold flowers from a cart. Acting casually as to not draw their attention, Amber Lee rose from her bench and sauntered in the opposite direction, sticking close to the storefronts. She had to get to Jedidiah and warn him before it was too late.

The whole situation was crazy. Amber Lee had no idea if the police were looking for her as a missing person or as a suspect. Maybe if she had gone to Internal Affairs right after her attack, the situation might be different. But now that she had threatened Pittman at gunpoint no one would side with her. *My God, what had she gotten herself into?*

Damn it all to hell. Pittman wasn't just going to turn the other cheek and let her get away with humiliating him in public. To be honest, he didn't seem all that thrilled that she was alive and okay. Amber Lee didn't trust Rosalind or Paul to tell her side of what happened. Unknowingly, she'd ruffled some feathers somewhere up high and it was now payback time. For now, it was best that she trusted no one in uniform.

Amber Lee reached the end of the block and turned the corner picking up her pace. Jedidiah had said he was going to be on Mims Street next to Mary Bishop Park. She hoped he was still there. She didn't know how to catch the underground railroad.

****

Amber Lee met up with Jedidiah in the park, next to the food trucks.

"Come on, we got to get out of here, fast."

"Why? What's going on?" Jedidiah fell in step with Amber Lee.

"The police are canvassing the area. They were showing photographs to the regulars on the street. Someone for certain is going to recognize me."

"We also got to be extra watchful of drones. The latest in spy technology."

"We need to get out of here."

"I know a guy that can give us a ride across town. We can spend the rest of the afternoon building our case down by the shipyards. No one will look for us there," Jedidiah said.

"We need to talk to Popson and Lynch."

"Pittman and Kauffman have probably given Popson and Lynch the heads up. They'll only stonewall us if we go to them. Rosalind, on the other hand, has a husband and three kids to think about. If we ever get anywhere close to making a case, I think she'll plea bargain for a lighter sentence."

"If I could somehow put pressure on Rosalind—try to get her to make a mistake."

"I know where we can get a car. We can tail her. Do you know where she lives?"

"Over on Gardner Street in the Mint Hill Apartment complex."

"I don't think we should approach her directly."

Chapter
Twenty

Through his connections, Jedidiah was able to borrow a twenty-year old faded, non-descript, four-door Toyota Corolla. The car was ugly but it ran smoothly. The tires were sound and his friend even filled the tank with gasoline.

Meanwhile, Amber Lee procured a 35mm camera and a prepaid cellular phone. Both the camera and phone were cheap and disposable.

The sky overhead was painted with dark clouds as the fugitives parked outside Rosalind's apartment in the rain. Their surveillance had begun.

Jedidiah shut off the car engine. "I guess if we're going to sit here in this tiny-made car, we have to talk about something." He left the key in the ignition just in case he had to make a quick startup.

"No politics, no religion, and no sexual fetishes. Everything else is on the table."

He smiled at her. "Have you ever done surveillance before?"

"A few times. Mostly conducted in a more favorable environment. An apartment across from a playground and an office building next to a pawn shop. Easy, breezy stuff like that."

"Did you have doughnuts and coffee?"

Amber Lee laughed. "How about pizza and Pepsi's. You watch too much television."

Jedidiah laughed with her. "Reporters have been known to snoop for a story. And I've done my fair share of time in the trenches."

"Did you have doughnuts and coffee?" Amber Lee teased.

Jedidiah made an ugly face. "Oh, hell no. More like sub sandwiches and bottled water."

They both laughed.

Jedidiah let the window down a little to allow in fresh air. The closed quarters had become hot and claustrophobic.

"I misjudged you," said Amber Lee, tilting her head upward to see into his eyes. "You seem to be a really nice guy. Sorry how things are going."

Jedidiah sensed that she genuinely meant what she said. He felt something of a bond with her. "It is what it is. You got nothing to be sorry about. In any case, you were just doing your job." He shrugged when he said it.

"I looked into your history. Do you still think about Erin?" Amber Lee was still staring at his face.

Jedidiah didn't answer right off. He looked away. The rain on the roof of the car made a peaceful backdrop. Finally, Jedidiah put words together that reflected his heart. "Yes. Everyday. Erin was my soulmate."

Amber Lee smiled. "Lucky girl to have loved you."

Outside the car, thunder cracked. The sky lit up with an electric blue flash.

"Yeah, lucky," said Jedidiah, almost to himself.

Two hours passed before Rosalind came out alone, dressed in a black raincoat with a red umbrella. While they watched, Rosalind climbed behind the wheel of a late model white GMC Yukon. Jedidiah started the Toyota and turned on the wipers. They followed Rosalind at a safe distance as she drove north on Hillex Drive.

Feeling paranoid, Jedidiah glanced into his rearview mirror several times to make sure he, too, wasn't being followed. For him to be pulled over for a traffic violation would be plain stupid.

"According to the funeral announcement, Rosalind and that murdered undercover Detective James Dubach are related, half brother and sister. You wanna bet Rosalind killed Sal out of revenge." He glanced over at Amber Lee for her answer. The time they put in surfing the Internet at the hotel had paid off.

"You might be right, but who ordered the bombing? And why?"

"I think Libertore ordered the bombing to shut Judge Crane and me up. He probably knew about Rosalind and her stepbrother; therefore, he knew the case against me was bogus. He might have moved for a mistrial."

Rosalind turned onto Southwick Street. Jedidiah followed. Six blocks later they arrived at Clancy Street. Rosalind pulled over and parked next to the Whale of a Fish Market. Jedidiah continued past and parked across the pier where he had a clear view of Rosalind's SUV. He and Amber Lee observed Rosalind step out of her Yukon without her umbrella and rush inside.

"I wonder why she came here," pondered Amber Lee. "Supposedly it was Sal who ordered her step-brother killed."

"I don't know. But Gomez and Montana may recognize me from the courtroom." Jedidiah turned to Amber Lee. "You better go inside."

"But what if Rosalind sees me. This is no good."

"I'll go. I'll put my ball cap down over my eyes. Hopefully no one will think twice because of the rain."

"Okay, but be careful."

"That, I will."

Jedidiah got out of the car and trotted across the street to the store. His heart pounded so loudly in his ears he didn't hear the eighteen-wheeler until it was right on him, its horn blaring. Jedidiah quickly stepped out of the way, slipping on the wet pavement. The rain showed no sign of letting up. He stopped for a minute to slow his breath and collect his wits before entering the door.

Inside the market, it was cold and rank with a fishy smell. Each section was marked with overhead signs. Jedidiah went in the direction of shellfish. He was looking over the fresh caught oysters when he spotted Rosalind talking heatedly with *Cockroach* Gomez and *Moose Dung* Montana. The three went into an office near the back and closed the door. Minutes later, Montana came out and waited at the front entrance. Jedidiah turned his back but watched over his shoulder to see whom Montana was waiting for.

Outside the front plate glass window, a late model white Corvette eased into a reserved parking slot. A middle-aged man dressed in a slicker and waterproof hat climbed out and joined Montana. After a brief discussion, the two men retreated to the office. In what seemed like forever to Jedidiah, the four came out. They were joined by two muscular-built men who were dressed like dockworkers.

Jedidiah discreetly snapped a picture of the group with the disposable camera. Pretending to be shopping, Jedidiah witnessed the raincoated man say something to the two brutes, whereas, they took Rosalind by the arms and forcefully led her out the rear of the store.

Jedidiah moved quickly trying not to attract the attention of the three conspirators. Once outside, he hurried across the street to the Toyota. When he opened the door, Amber Lee was slumped down in the passenger seat to avoid being seen. She sat up when Jedidiah climbed behind the wheel.

As he started the car, he updated Amber Lee on what was going on, "They forced Rosalind out the back of the store. I think they may be taking her some place she didn't want to go."

A white paneled van appeared from the rear of the building. Jedidiah and Amber Lee shielded their faces. The van sped past them and turned onto Southwick Street.

"I recognize one of those guys. He's the one who chased me off the freeway and on the sidewalk."

Jedidiah turned on the wipers and pulled out behind the van as it exited the pier. They were on the street, headed south out of town.

"Where do you think they're taking her?" asked Amber Lee.

"I don't know."

A short time later the van exited Southwick Street onto Highway Twenty-four. Six miles later, it exited on Canyon Road.

Jedidiah had an idea. "Wolf Mountain is about eight miles further up this road. If they plan on killing her, there's plenty of wooded area there to dump her body."

Amber Lee had an idea of her own. "Go around them and get there first. That way it won't look like we followed them."

"If that's not where they're going, we'll be screwed."

"Keep them in sight in your rearview. We'll see if they exit before then."

"All right, let's do it."

Jedidiah went around the van but kept it in his rearview. When they arrived at the park, the rain was starting to let up. He parked where they could see the front entrance, keeping the engine running. Because of the bad weather, attendance at the park was low. Still, there was a good chance they would go unnoticed. A short time later the van arrived.

"There it is," Jedidiah spoke excitedly. "We caught a break. I'll try not to get too close."

The park had several loose gravel roads leading off to different areas of interest. Horseback trails, campers, rental cabins, fishing and hiking were all accessible. The van came to a four-way intersection and braked. It turned the corner and continued.

"I've been up that way before," said Amber Lee. "That road leads to the cabins. We can hang back and see where they stop."

Jedidiah followed at a safe distance up the gravel road to a rustic cabin secluded deep in the trees where the van was parked in front. They continued as the two men led Rosalind, whose hands were behind her back, into the bungalow.

"Now what?" asked Jedidiah, parking in a clearing just beyond where they spotted the van.

"We have to flush them out and disable them."

"How do you suppose we do that?"

"We have to think of something. But listen, I don't want Rosalind to know I'm here." Amber Lee paced.

"Why not?"

"I'm not ready to face her just yet."

He shrugged. "If that's how you want to play it."

Amber Lee got an idea. "How about I hide behind the van while you distract them. When they come out, I'll take them down."

"You can do that without shooting them? I'm not up for killing anybody."

"I'm very efficient in the mixed martial arts."

"Those are some pretty big hombres."

"I can take care of myself. Just get them to come outside in the open where I can see them."

After Amber Lee took position behind the van, Jedidiah flung a large stone that bounced off the van's windshield, leaving a web-like crack. The loud thump could be heard inside the cabin. Seconds later, one of the longshoremen stepped out the door exhibiting a handgun. He looked left and right before moving down off the porch. As the rough-neck approached the van, Jedidiah watched Amber Lee jump out and knock the firearm out of the man's hand at the same time punching him in the face. Before he could react, Amber Lee side-kicked the stunned man in the knee, bringing him down. When he tried to stand, Amber Lee gave him a hopping sidekick to the face knocking him backwards. The surprised kidnapper regained his balance and pulled a switch-blade from his back pocket.

Jedidiah's heart almost stopped. The situation had gotten out of control.

"I got something for your skinny little ass. Ya crazy bitch." The burly man flicked the blade open, all the while smiling with swagger. Once again, he came at her and this time Amber Lee juked him while delivering a sidekick with all her strength underneath the chin.

From his position in the trees, Jedidiah heard the crunch of the man's jaw breaking. This time the man went down and stayed down on his back with his arms flung out. Amber Lee picked up his weapons, a Dymondwood with a four-inch blade and a Berretta M9. Both manufactured for no other purpose than to kill or do serious injury. She slipped them into the back pocket of her jeans. Amber Lee then drew her Glock and slowly advanced toward the front of the cabin. She signaled for Jedidiah to circle around to the rear.

Just as Jedidiah rounded the back of the cabin, the second captor exited through a rear door and sprinted across the wet grass toward the tree line.

Jedidiah yelled, "He's getting away out the back!" Jedidiah gave chase. He had no idea what he would do if the man had a gun.

Two hundred yards into the woods the runner came to a steep incline, too muddy for him to climb. Jedidiah caught up with him and stopped a short distance away. The cornered man drew a switchblade from his hip pocket. He flashed it at Jedidiah.

"Get the hell outta my way."

Jedidiah bent down and picked up a fallen tree limb. It wasn't much, but it was better than nothing. He could hear Amber Lee thrashing through the brush to catch up. She was close. He could only pray she was close enough. "I don't think so. You're gonna have to prove you can use that."

"It's your funeral, asshole." He started moving toward Jedidiah.

Jedidiah took a step backwards.

Before the attacker could come any closer, Amber Lee was there with her Glock aimed at his chest.

"Hold it right there, mister. Get your hands up and drop the knife."

The man dropped the switchblade to the ground and raised his arms. "What do you want? I ain't done nothing."

"Kick the knife over here," Amber Lee ordered.

He kicked the weapon toward Jedidiah, who picked it up. It was a four-inch Gerber. Jedidiah tossed the tree branch aside.

"What's your name? And why were you chasing me on the freeway the other day?" pressed Amber Lee.

"We were ordered to," answered the man cynically.

"By who?"

"Yeah, right," he snorted, shaking his head.

"Answer my questions."

"My name is Vargas. I ain't telling you nothing else."

"What were you going to do with that woman?"

"What woman?" Vargas asked sarcastically. The whole situation was now a joke to him.

"Oh, I'm crazy now. Answer my damn questions."

"Or you'll do what? Shoot me."

"I just might."

"I ain't telling you shit."

"Oh yeah. You can either get your ass over there on that fire ant mound or I can kick the crap out of you like I did your buddy. Either way, your gonna talk to us."

"You won't touch me without provocation. You're a cop."

"Ex-cop. You saw to that. I've already laid out your partner. You really need to talk before I start feeling like Ronda Rousey again. Be a damn shame to leave you up here sleeping on that fire ant mound."

He spat on the ground. "We were told to rough her up a little, you know, frighten her."

"Whose orders?"

"The hell with you. I ain't answering no more of your questions."

"Who was the third man with Montana and Gomez?" asked Jedidiah.

"Screw both of you."

Amber Lee turned to Jedidiah and motioned for him to move away. "Stand back, you don't want blood splatter on your clothes."

Vargas saw that she was serious. "All right. His name is Madison."

"Speak up," ordered Amber Lee. "I didn't hear you."

"Carl Madison. I hear he launders money for the operation. Now that's all I know."

"Come on, let's go. Start walking."

They led Vargas back to the cabin. Jedidiah retrieved nylon zip ties from inside the van. He tied Vargas and the unconscious man to a nearby oak tree.

Amber Lee used Vargas's cell phone to call 911. "I need help out here, ASAP. A woman has been kidnapped by two men."

"Where's your location, ma'am?" asked the emergency operator.

"Wolf Mountain. The third log cabin on Beaver Dam Trail. Please hurry!"

Amber Lee ended the call. She turned to Jedidiah and said, "We got to get out of here, fast."

****

Jedidiah and Amber Lee headed back to the rooftop after returning the Toyota to its owner. Before heading back to the rooftop, they stopped briefly at Flo's Diner for coffee. The local news station was just signing on air.

"Good evening. I'm Deborah Meyers, thank you for tuning in to Eyewitness News at Eleven. Our breaking story tonight has the police puzzled. One of Carver City's own detectives was found this afternoon, bound to a chair inside a cabin at Wolf Mountain. Two men, Anthony Vargas and Justin Harrah, were also found on the property secured to an Oak tree. According to hospital records, Justin Harrah had been severely beaten. Not much else is known as to why the detective was held hostage and who apprehended the two men. A police spokesperson tells eyewitness news that the

detective was unharmed and has returned home to her family. The two kidnappers, Vargas and Harrah, are being held in police custody with a bail hearing scheduled for tomorrow morning. Police say a woman called 911 and told them of the location of the kidnapping. That call was traced to Vargas's cellphone. Eyewitness News has reporters at the jailhouse and we will continue to bring you updates on this story as soon as they break."

After finishing their coffee, Jedidiah and Amber Lee left the diner and started the trek back to the rooftop. Now that the rain had stopped, many other couples were out enjoying the cool night breeze.

"The way Jacob Ross took on Libertore was, he collected the information on all the different players and forwarded it to different news agencies and magazines. After that, the authorities got involved. We can do better than that now by using social media."

Amber Lee moved closer. Jedidiah reached down and took ahold of her hand. Immediately, he felt a stirring in his loins.

Amber Lee gazed up at Jedidiah. "So basically, what you're saying is, Rosalind will have to explain why she went to the fish market while off duty to meet with suspects in an ongoing murder case. And why she was later found tied up in a mountain cabin."

"Exactly. And her two kidnappers are out on a limb in their roles. Why they were tied up and the one being beating to a pulp." Jedidiah squeezed Amber Lee's hand. "Remind me not to ever pick a fight with you."

They both laughed.

"Pittman will look incompetent having a fugitive detective under his command mixed up in corruption his department wasn't investigating," added Amber Lee.

"Since he has two detectives involved, it could get kind of rough on him."

Amber Lee suddenly became serious. "Serves him right. I hope he craps his pants when Internal Affairs come after him."

"He just may do that." Jedidiah laughed aloud. Without thinking about it, he drew Amber Lee against him. He was relieved when she didn't resist. He gave her a spontaneous full kiss on the lips. Again, she didn't pull away. The rest of the walk back to the rooftop he harbored conflicting emotions. Was he really ready to move on from Erin? Or was he just taking advantage of the situation? Amber Lee was a cop and he was a fugitive. He decided to take it a step at a time and see what fate awaited.

That following day Jedidiah texted April Winehouse at the *Post* a picture of Carl Madison talking with Gomez and Montana while Vargas and Harrah stood next to Rosalind. In the text Jedidiah warned Winehouse that Kauffman was involved and not to be trusted.

Chapter

Twenty-one

The thing about a lie is, it doesn't care who tells it. A lie doesn't care how its told, whether it be a bold-faced lie or a little white lie. Yet, at the end of the day, a lie is always exposed by the truth. Truth doesn't always guarantee justice but it does demand to be heard. When the news hit Carver City that an award-winning reporter and a dedicated young detective were being framed, and their reputations were being soiled by their department heads, people took to the streets in protest. The media worked diligently for a cover story. Everyone connected to Sal Hernandez's business operations lawyered up. Deceptions and even bigger mendacities trickled down from Centre Tower as *The Post* newspaper owners set out to cover their own ass. For a brief moment in time, truth had been overshadowed by fake news, but now, truth had arisen and she demanded to be examined.

Nearly a dozen television reporters and cameramen stopped the four Robbery-Homicide detectives on the courthouse steps as they left Vargas and Hurrah's bail hearing. It was hot as a Carolina Reaper chili pepper outside, but no one seemed to be affected except the Captain of Detectives. Sweat poured down Pittman's spine like an open faucet.

The questions came at once from all directions. "One female detective is missing from Third Street Precinct and her female partner was kidnapped by mobsters. Are the two cases related?" shouted a female newsperson with MSNBC.

"I can't speak on an open investigation," stated Pittman, trying to look official, but he came off looking artificial. Behind him stood Detectives Marshall, Stevenson, and Detective Senior Grade Jamison. Each wore dark shades and similar grim expressions.

"Who made the 9-1-1 call from Wolf Mountain?" asked a female newsperson from the *Times*.

Pittman turned his head to the reporter and answered, "We don't know at this time."

A male correspondent from CNN asked, "Who attacked the kidnappers?"

Pittman turned to face the man. "We don't know that either at this time."

"What do you know?" shouted a sarcastic female voice from the back of the group.

Pittman ignored the remark.

"How long have you known Detective Amber Lee was a victim and not a suspect?" asked the reporter from MSNBC.

Instead of answering the MSNBC reporter, Pittman turned his attention to a young man who held a local news affiliate microphone and nodded at him to speak.

The young journalist spoke up, "Both Harrah and Vargas have lawyered up and aren't talking. What is the department going to do now?"

"We have all our available resources committed to this issue. We hope to know more soon."

"Are Montana and Gomez going to be charged with ordering the kidnapping of the detective?" asked a CNN special correspondent.

"The department can't say for sure how deeply Mr. Montana and Mr. Gomez are involved. The DA's office will know the answer to that."

The MSNBC newsperson was diligent and pressed the captain further. "What role does Carl Madison play in this? In the photo printed in *The Post* today, Madison is in the fish market with Hector Gomez, Juan Montana, Anthony Vargas and Justin Harrah while the detective is being restrained. And do you have any idea where that picture came from?"

Pittman had had enough and abruptly ended the press conference. "This case will not be tried in the press. I have nothing more to say at this time."

****

The Post Editor, Scott Kauffman and the woman with him stopped in surprise, as radio and television news hounds and cameramen rushed at them as the two of them were leaving the Centre Tower building. The feeding frenzy had begun.

Kauffman felt like fresh meat in shark-infested waters. To make matters worse, he had no idea which way to swim for safety. Every direction he turned, the Washington story was blowing up in his face. Margo Spinner from KBTV stepped in to block their path. "Why was Jedidiah Washington let go from the *Post?*" she asked, before shoving her mic into Kauffman's face.

"Budget cost," he managed to mumble, avoiding eye contact with the cameras.

A male journalist from *Reuters* disputed that statement. "That's not what Washington is saying. He said a new sponsor wanted him out and you obliged."

"That's not true," Kauffman almost shouted, taking his coworker by the arm. He attempted to step around the man.

A correspondent from the *Associated Press* with the nametag Benson intervened, "*The Post* immediately took on that client after Washington's departure."

Kauffman felt like he was going to be nauseous. "That doesn't make what Washington said true."

"That doesn't make what he said a lie, either," retorted April Winehouse joining the huddle. She glared critically at her boss and the sales executive before adding, "Doesn't this look like what Jedidiah warned you about. The workings of a secret society?"

Before Kauffman could muster an answer, an aggressive afro-sporting female wearing a Black Lives Matter tee shirt shoved her way in front of him. "Why is Washington feeding negative info to the press about you if it isn't true?"

Kauffman stammered in confusion. More questions came at him faster than he could keep up with. All he could see were cameras and microphones. Without warning or excuse, the editor took ahold of the woman's arm and led her hurriedly to his car. Even as they drove away, newshounds continued to hurl questions at him. Life as he knew it, with the private dinners, lavish drinks, and open-ended expense accounts, was over.

Chapter
Twenty-two

The late-model stretch limousine pulled up next to the curb at the corner of Westgate and Temple Springs Avenue and shut off its lights. The affluent neighborhood was a showcase of Rolls Royce, Lamborghini, Bentley, Hummer, and Aston Martin automobiles. The extended Lincoln would blend in. The bodyguard-slash-chauffer kept the engine running.

Seated in the back, Bhoot smoked a Cuban cigar and reflected.

Police districts everywhere in the world had boxes of open case files that could be compared to their boxes of closed cases. Unless it was a close family member, or someone with an open grudge, finding and convicting a murderer was serious work. Television detectives made it look simple in that a murder could be wrapped up in sixty minutes. On the Lifetime network, beautiful, young housewives solved complex murder cases in between baking cookies and their next yard sale. In real life, people go missing all the time. Many of them never turn up. Their cases never closed. He knew this better than anyone.

Judge Crane had entrusted in a close friend that he believed Jedidiah Washington to be innocent and was being framed. Crane believed many of the jurors felt the same. Sanctions were ordered to silence Crane and Washington by Libertore leaders that he carried out. It was he who orchestrated the courthouse bombing.

Bhoot watched the dark silhouette step from the shadows and approach the rear of the vehicle. He pressed the button to unlock the door and the man climbed inside. As the limo pulled away from the curb, the interior lights slowly faded on. The passenger looked on in silence as the partition glass rose from behind the front seat up to the cushioned roof.

The passenger turned to his host and said, "So, we meet again, Bhoot."

Bhoot smiled warmly at his guest. "Thank you for joining me, Reddick. This meeting won't take long." Steven Reddick was an ex-CIA agent who now freelanced as a *Cleaner* for Libertore. Bhoot had great confidence in his ability.

"My time is your time."

Bhoot shrugged politely. "Very well. Pour a drink while I discuss your next assignment."

Reddick poured himself a small tumbler of Crown Royal and settled back holding the drink. It was good to execute the game plan before celebrating.

Bhoot got straight to the point, "A representative of our society has been compromised. His name is Carl Madison. He must be burnt a.s.a.p. to make our ugly situation disappear."

"What do you want me to do?"

"A high-profile murder case and bombing need to go away."

"You're asking me to credit Madison with the courtroom bombing and Sal's murder?"

Gone was the warm smile. Replaced now with thin lips and an icy glare. "You're not asked to credit him anything, Mr. Reddick. Make it all disappear. Tonight."

"I'll need money. Lots of it."

"No need to worry. All expenses are covered, Mr. Reddick. Equipment and supplies have been gathered and delivered to your room at the Ritz Carlton."

"Consider this case closed."

Chapter
Twenty-three

As soon as Reddick got to the Ritz Carlton and checked into his room, he went to work. First, he had an associate take and bury Sal Hernandez's missing murder weapon in Carl Madison's back yard. Using his laptop, Reddick used a RAT to hack into the computers at Whale of a Fish and Madison's uptown office. He preferred the Remote Access Trojan DarkComet software to Metasploit Pro and Kali Linux. Each hacker had his or her own style. Posing as an IT specialist made it easy for him and his team to install LogMein on a client computer.

When the opportunity presented itself, Reddick was able to gain access remotely. It didn't take but an hour for him to doctor the Whale of a Fish financial account to appear as if they were cooking the books. Next, he used AirCrack-ng software to break the security key in Madison's wireless adapter and plant fake correspondence to make it look like Madison had planned the bombing on the courthouse. Using Kali Linux NetHunter software Reddick managed to get inside Madison's phone and plant a Trojan horse. Now he had access to the finance guru's conversations with his attorney. Hector Gomez, Juan Montana, Anthony Vargas, and Justin Harrah would all get jail time for running a crooked operation and kidnapping. Carl Madison, on the other hand, would probably spend the rest of his life in jail for the murder of Sal Hernandez and ordering the courtroom bombing.

Madison wasn't stupid enough to think he could make a deal with the Justice Department and enter the Witness Protection Program. That would be suicide for him and his family. Libertore was everywhere. The person you least suspect could be a member. It was in Madison's best interest to keep his mouth shut and do the time.

The dilemma with cutting the head off the snake was first locating the snake. Especially if the general public believed the snake didn't exist. The world awoke to a new and more challenging crisis every morning. The Hernandez murder and courthouse bombing were yesterday's news with American's short attention span. With the murder case solved, Jedidiah Washington would be released from jail after serving whatever time the courts imposed on him for escaping. Amber Lee would be re-instated on the police force. If they were smart, there would be no more talk of a secret society where critical decisions were executed in the shadows.

Reddick shut down the laptop and poured himself a stiff tumbler of whiskey. He settled back on the bed to watch classic movies on the hotel television. The Cleaner preferred porn but high-end hotels had become so correct these days.

It was now time to celebrate.

Chapter
Twenty-four

The next day Carl Madison was arrested and charged with the murder of Sal Hernandez and ordering the courthouse bombing that killed fourteen people and injured nine others. Madison quickly hired an attorney and pleaded not guilty. In the meantime, crime scene investigators unearthed the revolver used in the murder, buried in Madison's backyard next to the pool house.

Hearing the news of Madison's arrest, Jedidiah and Amber Lee both came out of hiding. Together they entered the Third Street Precinct and turned themselves in to the watch captain, who quickly alerted the station commander, the chief of police, the city attorney, and the mayor. Within half an hour, the gathering was moved to the conference room. After an extensive interrogation where neither Jedidiah nor Amber Lee gave up their collaborators, the dignitaries left. Jedidiah and Amber Lee were at the front desk with Captain Mason.

"Where's Rosalind Kelly? Is she here today?" Amber Lee asked Mason. A number of uniformed officers and detectives stood around staring at the couple.

"Detective Kelly put in for family leave, which was approved on yesterday. She's getting rest before coming back full time." He then lowered his voice, "We just learned that one of the undercover detectives that Hernandez had butchered, was her half-brother. She was conducting her own investigation into his murder."

Amber Lee glanced around at the onlookers. "Where's Captain Pittman? I haven't seen him."

The Captain stuffed some papers into a folder before dropping it in a file cabinet. He closed the drawer and turned back around. "Pittman was granted early retirement. His last day is next Friday."

Amber Lee led Jedidiah to the break room where they found a table away from the main traffic. Every eye in the room was trained on them.

"I hear the department plans to drop all conspirator charges on me," said Amber Lee.

"The city attorney said I may be locked up to for escaping jail. If I'm charged with a misdemeanor, I could get up to twelve months. If I'm charged with a class C felony, it could be anything over a year."

Jedidiah looked Amber Lee in the eyes. There was so much he wanted to say to her. But not now. "I want to thank you for standing with me. I would never have gotten the evidence without you."

Amber Lee blushed. "It was my pleasure."

They sat for a moment in silence. Amber Lee looked around at the people staring at them. Turning back to Jedidiah she asked, "Do you still think Libertore exist?"

"Yes. Even more so."

She shrugged her shoulders. "Why?"

"All the evidence just suddenly came together. The trail was wiped clean to end with Madison."

"If that were true, why doesn't he call them out?"

Jedidiah lifted his shoulders. "Call who out? Are you kidding? They'd kill him first."

"Why haven't they tried to kill you?"

"Because I don't know anything. I'm just an ex-reporter with an axe to grind. Madison on the other hand, knows too much. And he knows the score is against him. He won't talk."

Amber Lee cupped both hands on the table. "So, you're back where you started."

"Yes, but at least without murder charges hanging over me."

"Will you go after them again?" Amber Lee searched Jedidiah's eyes for an answer.

Jedidiah reached out and took hold of her hands. "I'd rather pursue you. That's if you'll have me. You know, a policewoman dating a criminal."

Amber Lee burst into a fit of laughter. "Shit, who cares."

You can find more books by
Harvey Butaleon Degree Sr.
at Amazon.com or visit:
www.inazone.net

Made in the USA
Columbia, SC
10 December 2022

73399051R00054